THE PROVISIONER

Rhyd Wildermuth

THE PROVISIONER

Rhyd Wildermuth

ISBN: 978-1-7357944-6-4

RITONA a.s.b.l
3 Rue de Wormeldange
Rodenbourg, Luxembourg L-6955

Layout and Design: Rhyd Wildermuth

View our catalogue and online journal at
ABEAUTIFULRESISTANCE.ORG

For Ralph,
for the last wolf of Luxembourg,
for the wolves who returned,
for all the other wolves of the Ardennes,
and for Arduinna.

CHAPTER ONE

Knock.

Garen woke to a pounding on the door and a pounding in his head.

"Coming," he groaned. Breathing in, he inhaled a scent he wasn't expecting. He forced his eyes open against the protest behind them.

"Again?" grunted a voice close to his ear.

Garen didn't recognize the voice. He didn't recognize the rafters above him, the pattern of morning light illuminating motes of dust where there shouldn't be dust at all.

Also, *it smelled like horse shit.*

He sat up before turning to look at his companion. Hairy, a little older than himself. Muscled scarred body, a soldier or a workman, not a merchant or scholar. Unkempt, musky, bearded. Not the worst he'd woken next to.

"What?" the man grumbled, meeting Garen's gaze. His eyes were grey, distant. A bit feral.

Garen answered. "There's someone at the door."

The man sat up. Garen stared at his body, the sweat-matted fur of his chest reminding him of a wet dog.

"What door are you talking about, mate?" His voice was gravelly, low-timbred. His breath was raw with old wine, but no rot.

Knock.

Garen turned away, back towards the knocking, his head revolting at the sudden movement. He blinked back the pain, then blinked again. He could see no door.

"We're in a stable, remember?"

"That's the smell," Garen grunted. "I don't remember a thing."

The man grinned, reaching out his arm.

Garen didn't recoil at his touch. "What's my name?"

Worn, calloused fingers grazed Garen's jaw. "You wouldn't tell me last night. You seriously don't remember?"

Laughing, enjoying the feel of the man's hand running through his stubble, he answered. "No. I mean, I know my name." Then, noting what look like offense sweep over the man's face, he added, "and I'm sure you were great."

The man shook his head. "I'd knock you around sober too, mate."

Knock.

The pounding on the door came again, louder. A voice now: *We need a Provisioner.*

Understanding pierced Garen's mind, hard. "I gotta go, mate."

"Name's Sorn."

Garen stood up. "Sorn. Okay. I'm Garen, though I probably shouldn't tell you that if I wouldn't last night."

"Garen, right. You did, I just forgot too. We drank a lot."

By the way the world spun around him and his head threatened to explode, Garen was certain the man was right. "Sorn. Great. Uh, where are we?"

"The stables by the docks. Ruynstreet."

Not a long walk, then…Garen could get back before they arrived. "Good. Uh, see you again maybe?"

Sorn rose to stand in front of him. Erect, his body hair still matted with sweat, his serious, seeking eyes staring back at him as Garen scanned the man's body.

"Yeah. Maybe. Your clothes are still soaked, probably."

A few seconds passed before his words came back to him —this man, Sorn, was beautiful. "Uh…it rained last night?"

Sorn laughed and pointed to where Garen's trousers hung, dripping on a wall hook. "You jumped into the river to get your shirt."

"Why was my shirt in the river?"

Slapping out the still-sopping wet fabric, Sorn shrugged. "You threw it. You…you were really drunk, mate."

"Yeah," Garen answered, holding his head. "I think you're right."

Knock.

Trudging shirtless in wet boots and trousers through the dawning streets of the city, Garen was miserable. He was cold, his legs chafed against the soaked cloth, his boots squeaked and splashed water across the cobbles with every step.

Whatever he'd done the night before had been stupid. Reckless. He maybe shouldn't have told Sorn his name. He maybe shouldn't need to hurry cold and wet through back streets to his room. He also, maybe, wanted to go back to the stables instead.

His head hurt. He'd drank too much. He remembered nothing.

Knock

Another blackout. When did it start? He couldn't piece it together. He'd had dinner. Done some writing. Lit the candles.

"Fuck," he muttered aloud, walking faster. Had he blown them out? Had he burned down the house? The fear made him dizzier, the pounding now like a hammer rather than a knocking.

Knock

No. They wouldn't be knocking on his door if there were no door to knock on. The house hadn't burned down. Maybe he'd blown the candles out before he left, or maybe they'd burned out of their own accord. Worst he might find was a wax-covered altar, a ruined prayer mat.

We need a Provisioner.

"I'm coming, damn it" Garen shouted at the empty alley, his voice echoing off waking stone. He'd seen no one; the city still slept, no vendors or city watch to gawk at his wet clothes and shivering, naked chest.

The quicker pace was a bad idea. He stopped to retch into a corner, his throat burning as he choked out something that smelled of wine, apple liquor, and possibly beer.

He leaned his head against the wall, spitting out the acrid bile. The chill of the stone eased his headache some. He was still shivering, but the cold made him feel feverish, too.

"Didn't see this coming," he said to himself, chuckling at the irony.

He retched twice more before arriving home. No one stood in front, no horses were tethered outside. He fumbled in the pocket of his trousers for the key, then cursed when he found it gone.

He'd climbed the garden wall plenty of times before, though never while so drink-sick. The jolt from landing on the other side seared more pain through his skull, but he ignored it. He stopped at the rain barrel to drown his head and wash some of the wine-vomit from his face.

The cold water quickened his senses a bit. Garen heard the noise he was waiting for. Shod-hooves over cobble, three —maybe four—sets. Still distant, but approaching fast. He didn't have much time.

He hoisted himself up to the edge of the rain barrel, grabbed the ledge above him. His balance was off, he almost tipped the barrel. His wet boots made gripping near-impossible, his fingers were cold and raw. Each jarring move threatened the temporary truce his stomach had made with his head. Just before he'd lifted himself to the window, he retched again.

The window was open. He'd foreseen at least one thing, though he still didn't remember anything after lighting the candles. Once his left knee had purchase on the ledge, he threw himself through, landing on the floor by his bed.

He lay there for a few seconds, facing the low table where the candles from last night still glowed and flickered.

Knock, he heard, this time in-time.

He stared at the icon between the candles before blowing them out. She-Who-Foresees stared back, placid, calm, wise. Indifferent.

Knock, he heard again.

He didn't remove his eyes from the painting as he stood, kicked off his boots, peeled off his trousers. As angry as he was, the icon calmed him. Black eyes, gold skin, vestments of blue and green on a black background. Beautiful and distant, gazing upon worlds not yet born. Watching. Preparing.

"What'd you do to me?" he demanded, then caught himself. His words sounded wrong. Ungrateful.

Naked and wet and shivering, Garen remembered what came next. He turned from the shrine, dried himself off quickly with a thick blanket, and then wrapped it around himself before running downstairs.

Knock, he heard, just as he reached the door.

His key was still in the lock. He'd left without it, must have actually left by the same window he entered this morning. He'd been really not his own.

Garen turned the key, lifted the second latch, opened the door just as the heavily-armed man on the other side said:

"We need a Provisioner."

"I know," he answered.

CHAPTER TWO

Garen didn't raise his head from the steaming tea in front of him. "I'm told I went swimming last night."

Yura clucked her tongue. "And came out dirtier than you went in, sure. Who was he?"

He managed a short laugh. "Uh, I don't really know. He seemed nice enough."

The woman's voice softened. "She sent you off blind a second time, huh? Praise and scorn be upon Her."

His teacher's irreverence usually irked him, but this time Garen welcomed it. "Third time. This guy was beautiful, though." He sipped some of the tea she'd poured him. It was bitter, tasted of tree bark and dirt. "If I hadn't heard them coming, I'd still be there trying to do something I'd actually remember."

Yura tousled his hair a bit, then smelled her hand and scowled. "You smell as awful as you look. She-Who-Foresees wouldn't have it any other way. I'm gonna draw you a bath, and then you're gonna tell me what they're wanting with you."

The imminence of a bath relaxed him. "Yes, please." Then, remembering the weave of their demands, he sighed and added: "they've banned me. I can't tell you."

The woman rose up full, laughed loudly. "No man's ever stopped me yet, Garen. Drink your tea and stop cowering."

"I'm not..." he started, but she'd already left the room. "...Cowering" he muttered to himself, breathlessly. His head forward, his shoulders hunched, his arms guarding his chest as if expecting to be hit.

He *was* cowering. He sat up straight, let himself breathe again.

As he finished his drink-sick tea, as he stood and walked to where the bath waited for him, as he undressed and let his body adjust to the heat of the water, and as he sank into the fragrant water of the bath, Garen tried to piece together the last sixteen hours.

The usual dread had come upon him last night. Couldn't focus long enough to cook anything, so he'd gotten herbed meat and bread at a street vendor. Eaten only half of it, gave the rest to an urchin, wandered back to his rented room.

He'd tried to write. Nothing had come. He had no attention for the stack of unread books he'd bought three weeks before, had no errands, no friends he wanted to see. Not tired either, he'd lit candles at the small shrine and sat, staring.

He remembered nothing after, before waking next to Sorn in the stables. He had gone swimming in the river with his boots on to fetch a shirt he'd thrown in. He'd fucked a horse-keeper —no. The man had been too strong, possibly a dock worker, maybe even a mercenary.

He remembered none of that. Where'd they even meet? Garen never drank at the docks—too many soldiers, too far to walk home drunk at night without being stopped.

This morning—the men, the pronounced demand, woven with a ban. He remembered nothing they'd said. Yura was right —he'd been cowering. What they needed a Provisioner for had terrified him, but now he couldn't even remember.

The last day made little sense to him, the weeks before were even less clear. Autumn had come, nights colder, days shorter, city quieting as if waiting for death. Perhaps it was: war loomed, lightness of living smothered by foreign threats and panicked rulers.

The world around him felt distant and cold, so too his own world. He'd fought with his landlord over a rent-rise. Estranged a few friends with arguments, stupid politics, his impatience with their lack of thought. Had few friends left now. No lover, no desire to find more of either, at least when conscious.

Yura had warned him about the demands of She-Who-Foresees. "You can become a Provisioner without her," she'd told him, "and not find out the next day you were running naked through the hex markets screaming that they're all frauds."

"That happened to you?" Garen has asked, fascinated.

"Ayup. They were, too, but that don't make the embarrassment much better. I don't have the kind of body people want to see flopping around in the street."

He'd laughed. She looked great for someone past sixty. Then he'd remembered: he heard about this, a year before coming to her for training. "Wait! That was you?"

She nodded, solemn-serious. "And it'll be you if you start try-ing to see like She sees. Though I dare say there'd be a lot more would want to see you flopping about."

Sitting in the tub, remembering, Garen laughed. He'd not been found naked in the streets yet. But walking home wet, shirtless, wasn't too far away.

Dried, dressed, he stared at himself in the mirror. He didn't look so awful now. Tired, though. Needed to shave, needed to cut his hair. Maybe wouldn't do either, let both grow longer. Maybe a beard with his face, a beard like Sorn had. Now into his twenties—perhaps time to grow up.

This thought amused him. Friends joked he was an old man. Cranky, stubborn. Boring. Kept to himself too much, read too much, drank not enough. Too serious. Too content to stare into a distance than dance in the fleeting now.

"I'm going to stop shaving," Garen said, entering the kitchen.

"And how long you been thinking that one through?" Yura teased. She filled two plates, handed them to him, stared hard into his left eye: "Or is that part of the demand?"

He shook his head. "I don't think so. I just thought maybe it'd look good."

Bemusement in her voice. "Of course it will. Let's eat, boy. You're always too serious when you're hungry."

Her banter lightened his mood. They sat next to each other

at the table, plates in spaces they cleared of clutter.

"So they came when?" his teacher asked, still chewing her last bite of lamb.

Garen swallowed, drained a cup of water. "A little after dawn. I heard them coming in the stables."

Shaking her head hard, the rings on her ears clanging, she asked him, "So you ran back home from a man to meet those soldiers?"

"Uh...yeah," he answered. "Is that weird?"

She grunted. "You heard them coming."

"About an hour before, yes."

She followed a silence with a sigh: "She told you."

He returned his own pause. Then, "I don't know. I heard them knocking, and so I ran home to get there before they showed up."

Yura stood. Dropped her fork on her plate, loud. "That took me ten years to learn. You're... She picked you well."

He raised his head to meet her uncomfortable awe. "You picked me, Yura. And taught me really well."

She walked from the room, returned with a candle and a bowl of water. "You showed up at my door all burning with sight and fear. I wasn't gonna turn you away. But I definitely didn't choose you for anything. Maybe She didn't either, but saw ahead what you could do. I don't think it matters, in the end."

She placed the bowl on the table. He watched her, thought on her words. He saw sense there.

"You still not talking to Her?" he asked.

"Nope. Three months now. I'm too old to be running around

outside time like I've got all the time in the world." She lit the candle, sank its weighted end into the bowl. "If She wants more of my time, She's gotta give me more of my own."

Garen stayed silent, watched the flame play on the surface of the water. He'd known Yura for four years, heard each of her stories about She-Who-Foresees. Each tale fascinated more, filled him with more desire. He'd wanted to meet Her. Begged Yura to teach him the devotions, the prayers, the dream-chants, the ways to find Her in the threshold, the realms between wake and sleep.

He had not understood why not, why a Provisioner would not take her patronage. Sent running naked through a hex-market, sure; found swimming in a river mid-autumn, of course. But still, why not? Why not, when She could end the nightmares, teach control of the sight, a chance to avoid un-timely death?

Yura told him at midsummer that she was done. She would speak no longer to their Lady. He had thought she joked.

"Nope. All done. No more. She can find someone else."

Stuttering he'd replied: "but why? What happened?"

She'd shrugged. "Nothing. I'm just done. Maybe forever. If Se wants me, she knows where to find me, and She knows what's She's gotta do to earn my favor back."

Such talk had made him bristle. The first time She-who-fore-sees had spoken, he was hers. All doubts, all fears: gone. Years of headaches, nightmares, walking-sleep: ended.

Yura taught him to find her, with warnings. "She's pushy,

She's got no boundaries, She doesn't take no lightly. You gotta push back or you lose yourself."

He found no need to push. Finding Her, he found himself. Her presence was peace, sleep after a long day with no urgency to wake the next. She gave sense to everything, asked nothing in return.

※

Yura's voice woke him from these thoughts. "You seeing this?"

Garen searched for fragments of visions, dance of light on water. "I don't see anything."

Yura nodded. "No reflection of the flame. It just...disappears into the water."

He shifted, looked again. She spoke the truth. The water reflected no light. "That's...that's bad, right?"

Yura rubbed her eyebrows. "I've never seen that before. Could be their ban. Could be something worse. Could just be we're tired. When...when they got you going?"

Garen sunk in his chair. "Three days from now. I have to gather provisions and be ready at dawn on sixth-day."

Yura met his eyes. Hers were kind, concerned. Worried. "And you're going blind, huh? She and I might not be speaking ever again, but...well, you know what you gotta do. You gotta ask Her."

He nodded. He'd just won a long argument with Yura, but it felt nothing like victory.

CHAPTER THREE

Evening light illuminated the surface of the river as Garen walked from Yura's house. The water ran slow, sluggish. The late autumn rains not yet begun; summer had been dry and hot. The stone of ancient embankments bared themselves below newer river-walls: bleached sandstone above sludge-greyed marble, lain in the reigns of richer kings.

He trudged slowly, listened to the lowered water lap against the stone. The streets were empty despite the hour, gaslights dimmed, stars still unseen. The world was distant, empty: he a ghost in a city that marked not his passing.

Though cured by Yura's tea and a long day of sleeping, his head pounded with thoughts. Fear. His teacher's seeing had failed. She could give him no comfort nor direction for his first provisioning. Years before he looked towards this day, certain he'd need no advice. Now, without her help, he was terrified.

He remembered little from the morning's demand. They needed a Provisioner. Diviners chose him over others. He would fulfill his obligation to the king or forfeit his life. Simple terms, no ambiguity, no escape.

They gave three days to prepare, without word for what he was to prepare. They told him where to meet them; they would depart the city upon his arrival.

He did not even know who they were.

Yura had provisioned six times in her life, her other students twenty times between them. She'd said none of those provisionings involved such secrets. "We used to find *them*, you know. None of this them-demanding-us sort of thing. Things have changed. Now, they just come around telling you what you gotta do. I don't like this."

Her words echoed in his fear-filled head. He knew the history, how once authorities honored and feared Provisioners. Now they were only tolerated when they served the empire.

"On forfeit of your life," the demand had said. He did not tell Yura this. She would have raged.

Lost in his thoughts, he'd missed a turn. He'd been walking too far along the river, a longer route. Garen stopped, looked for a street sign. He found one, read its faint letters in the dim light, and closed his eyes.

Ruynstreet.

Why'd he come back here? *He'd* not meant to. He'd not, anyway.

He was standing in front of the stables. "This is stupid," he muttered, even as his feet walked to the door.

"No," he whispered, watching his hand slip through the gap between masonry and wood, trying the latch.

Garen fumbled in the darkness, met the reek of horse and moldering straw with unbidden nostalgia. He could see nothing, no light filtered through the slate roof. "Sorn?" he called. His voice echoed back much louder than he'd hoped. "Hey —it's Garen. The guy from last night." He stilled his breathing, strained to listen for a rustle, a whisper, a snore.

Nothing.

Garen latched the door on his way out, tried to walk hard away from his stupidity. Of course Sorn wouldn't be there. Garen bit his lip as he tread the streets, biting even harder each time he threw a glance backward in empty hope.

He arrived home and stormed up the stairs to his room, throwing the door open with a crash. The world was a bitter place—it deserved no more of his kindness, and definitely none of his care. He threw himself into bed. Too tired to undress, too tired to light Her candles, too tired to fuck his hand, too tired for everything, and definitely too tired to dream.

Morning came, and with it a knock on the door of his room.

Garen didn't answer. The knock came again, and again, and again, then stopped. He listened as footsteps fell away, down the stairs, the heavy slow gait of his landlord.

Garen hadn't paid rent for two months after the rent-rise. He had the money, but intended to wear down the old man rather than give in. That was Yura's suggestion. She always chided him for how easily he bent his back to people above him, too eager to please them.

"I mostly don't want the trouble," he'd protested when she pressed him.

"Then you don't want life," she'd answered, not without kindness. "It's all trouble."

His landlord was an ass anyway. Prattled endlessly that immigrants were ruining the city, how the lords were never harsh enough with enemies. He'd prefaced the rent-rise with his blood thirst. "War's coming, and it's about time. And about time you pay what this room's worth."

"*War's coming.*" His landlord hadn't been the only one to say it. War was always coming, though—Garen couldn't remember a time when the land wasn't preparing for war. This time though it did seem like it would come. Soldiers everywhere, banners draping taverns and shops, covering windows, suspended from lamp-posts.

He remembered no time like this, nor did Yura when he asked. "There's a war coming, sure" she'd said. "It's not my war, and they better not try to make it mine, because I don't fight for anyone."

Garen had no intentions of fighting either. He'd not used his fist for something besides pleasure since becoming a man, had never held a sword not between a man's legs.

Sorn's. Garen remembered it. Bigger than his own, thicker, unhidden by the thick coat of dark hair around it. Limber, muscled legs, a mantle of fur cascading from his chest down his stomach. His face, though—almost animal, or at least more-than-human. Narrow grey eyes, piercing under thick brows, staring as if hungry.

Garen groaned. He'd not noticed he was thrusting into his fist, his hand wet and slick from cock-spit. A second later and he was panting, grunting, not bothering to stifle his voice as he came.

His shuddering woke him into life. He had provisions to gather, prayers to offer. He ran his hand through his hair. He got out of bed quickly, crossed the room to the shrine. He knelt, lit two new candles, and waited for Her answer.

Chapter Four

When Garen first met the Lady-of-provision, he'd almost died.

Yura had warned him not to try. She told him story after story of how She destroyed the lives of Her devoted, but each tale his teacher told made him want to meet Her more. So he'd gathered the candles and ground the resins, prepared the shrine, and prayed.

Nothing happened the first day, nor the second. This confused him, but the more he was met with silence, the more fervent he prayed. Those days became a week, and then another. He hadn't expected it to take so long, refused to leave the shrine except to piss and shit. He'd made no provisions for food, became weak eating stale bread and then crumbs and then nothing. He'd forget to drink water until his throat became so dry he couldn't pronounce the chants. One week, and then another, and then another, trying to prove his devotion to Her, trying to prove his worth.

He didn't know how much time had passed until Yura shouted at him, standing over his shaking, crouched body.

He'd given Yura a spare key when he first started training with her, not her request but his. He wanted to know someone might find his dead body one day, someone besides his landlord.

"Three weeks I haven't heard from you. And here you are covered in your own drool like our Lady's gonna talk to you if you look like a neglected baby."

"She hasn't found me worthy yet," he blathered. "I'll pray more."

Yura might have been old, but she was also really strong. She yanked him up by the arm, shouting "You'll do no such thing for anyone, lady or lord or lover. I'm putting you to bed."

By then, Garen had become too feeble to resist. She undressed him and he relented, helplessly. She threw him on the bed, and then wrapped his blankets around his body so he couldn't get up.

Just after, drifting into sleep, She arrived. A sense of gold and black, sun and shadow. And then green and blue, tree leaf and beyond it the sky. Then all four, light filtered through branches: hot, dappled with cold shade. He was before and after, staring from the end of time and from its beginning. Water made sense, and wind. He saw stars, was stars, stars dead yet still shining at their birth. He was time, stretching before and after, and She was there, someone, a presence close but very distant, touching him without body, echoing before any sound was ever made.

When he woke late that night, it was not from sleep but an endless ocean of time. He woke into his room, with Yura still sitting next to him.

He met Her. She had found him worthy. He told Yura this.

"That's what you think, boy? You're *worthy*? I'm a poor teacher if that's what you're getting from this."

Now Garen knew better. He didn't need to be worthy at all, only to listen. He lit his candles, chanted Her devotions, then relaxed. She couldn't be found in effort anymore than wind could be held in the hand. Seek grand visions and none come, grip tightly to threads and they snap.

He sat at Her shrine and waited. She would guide him to the provisions, would reveal what was needed, would wake into him what the future knows of the now.

She told him only one thing. Garen left the house to tell Yura what he learned.

❖

Yura stomped her feet, furious. "My wolf paw? How do you even know I have one?"

He shrugged. "You just told me. You wouldn't have said 'my wolf paw' if you didn't have one."

"Praise and screw Her," she huffed. "I do. And I don't want to think what She wants you with it."

Garen shrugged. "Did you ever know what you needed provisions for until you needed them?"

Yura sat, loudly. "No. 'Course not. I just—you know there haven't been wolves for more than a hundred years, right?"

Rubbing his hand against the coarse stubble of his beard, Garen told her no, he hadn't known that. "How'd you come by it then?"

"From my mother. From her mother. From her father to her mother, a hunter she never saw after the night her daughter was made."

"Oh" Garen replied, understanding the weight of his request. "That's a bit sacred to you then, huh?"

"Lady piss you, boy—you don't..." Yura's huff deflated in one loud exhalation. "Yeah. It's great-grandmother sacred."

"I can't ask you for that, Yura. I'm sorry."

"You already did, boy. And She wouldn't have told you it was needed if it weren't. And maybe my great-grandfather wouldn't have fucked my great-grandmother if She-Who-Foresees didn't want you to have a wolf paw. So, I wouldn't be here without you, you get it?"

Her logic was dizzying, but Garen saw she was right.

"This is how She works. You try to tell Her no and She comes up behind you almost a hundred years to get something from you."

Her face wasn't as flustered as her speech. Garen though he saw her look a little...wistful?

"Okay, okay. It's yours," she said. "You'll need it, I don't. I don't got a daughter to give it to, and you're the closest to a child I'll ever have, so it's time to pass it on. I'll go get it."

His teacher's emotion struck him hard. "Wait—Yura?"

She'd stood already, was walking out of the room, but turned. "What?"

"I...I'm honored you feel like I'm your son."

Yura grinned back at him. "Enough of this." Then, motioning for him to follow, she added, "I got some provisions for you."

Garen followed Yura into her shrine room. Warm from candles, smelling deep of incense. The small room always evinced the opposite emotion of his teacher: calm. He liked the room, also liked his teacher. What Garen didn't like was how she acted when she was in the room.

The room was full of spirits. Icons, seals, sigils, bits of bone and bird arrayed around candles and oil-flames. Heavy with the breathing otherworld, full of silent voices ready to speak. Garen couldn't unbid the awe from awakening when he entered, but Yura? Yura was rude.

"You bitch them out, or they stomp all over you" she'd said the first time he'd entered with her. And then, turning to a shrine, she'd spoken again. "You hear me? I'm a bitch, but I'm not your bitch."

She was less irreverent this time, though. "I did some forelooking for you. Talked to some I don't talk to no more."

The sudden tenderness startled Garen. If what she'd seen made her feel emotion at all, this provisioning was more serious than he feared.

Yura gestured throughout the room, pointing at the shrines. "They all gave me different answers. Never can usually agree, but this time— it's like they're all arguing with each other."

"Who did you ask?"

Yura shrugged. "All of 'em. Some don't want you to go. Some don't want me to help you. Others...", and here she pointed to her own shrine to She-Who-Foresees, "told me you're not coming back."

Garen felt the ground open beneath him. "She didn't say that to me."

"Course not!" Yura clucked. "You wouldn't have wanted to hear it from Her anyway." And then, turning to face him, her eyes deeply serious, she said, "and anyway She knows you wouldn't believe me if I told you, which is probably why She said it."

This didn't make Garen feel any better. He hadn't considered he might die. Unlike other Provisioners, he hadn't gotten a vision of his own death yet. Yura had told him it was usually the first vision they ever see.

"I'm going to die?"

"What's death?" Yura asked, suddenly laughing. "It's not coming back. But that doesn't mean you don't die again and again. We just don't leave a corpse 'till the last death."

Garen relaxed a little, remained silent.

"So you don't come back, and that's all good. But I see you again anyway somehow. That's something." Her face softened when she saw her student's grim stare. "Smile, boy. We survive everything until we don't."

She took something off one of the shrines and handed it to him, closed-fist. It dropped into Garen's hand and he stared at it, curious. A small, silver coin.

"You'll be needing this. My wolf paw's in my room. Well, your wolf claw now, I guess."

When Garen first found his way to Yura four years before, she'd been very, very unhappy to see him.

Fevered dreams haunted his sleep and waking for months. Nothing made sense, his life quickly fell apart. He couldn't keep work, his friends abandoned him. He smelled awful, but couldn't summon the focus for a bath.

He'd had no idea what was happening to him, didn't know why he woke in alleyways and parks, remembered nothing of the nights before. No one could help him, he'd become a walking ghost. And then one night he was at a strange door, Yura's door, soaking wet in a chill winter rain, knocking until she answered.

When she finally opened, she shouted at him. "I don't teach anymore. Go away"

Garen didn't go away. He couldn't. This open door, this woman before him, had made sense like nothing else had.

The old woman stomped her feet repeatedly, as if stamping out a fire on her doorstep. "Damn it. Go *away*. I told them I'm done."

Garen started to cry.

She shut the door.

How much longer he'd waited there, crying, he didn't remember. She'd opened the door again, started at him, stomped her feet again and barked, "get in out of the rain at least."

She'd taken pity on him. She'd lost arguments she'd been having with her spirits when he'd shown up dripping wet and crying at her door. That made her even more unhappy about it, but she was kind anyway.

She started training him, teaching him to put off the dreams until sleep, showing him how to make space for the unbidden visions. "Make space for them and they can't jump you," she'd said, though it took several more weeks for Garen to know what—and who—'they' were.

"You're a Provisioner, I'm sorry to say." When she said those words, it'd been the first time Garen had heard of such a thing.

"You know when you just happen to have the very thing someone needs? Like, when someone needs to write something and you happen to have a pen on you, or you find some coins on the ground and it just happens to be the amount someone else needed to borrow to buy their dinner, or when someone mentions they lost their dog and you happened to see the pup running down the street earlier that day?"

"Luck, yeah" Garen answered. "Coincidence."

"Nope. *Provisioning.* You provide for folks because you saw something that you just sort of knew would be needed later. You didn't know, really, or not like you know where you live or what your name is. But you definitely know."

Garen shook his head. "That happens to everyone though."

Yura clicked her teeth. "Sure. But they got no say in it. Provisioners do. We can see what's going to be needed for others before it's needed, and follow the stream of a thing to where it meets up with the river of a person."

That made no sense to him then. She tried several other ways of explaining: hints to stories that haven't been written yet, buying the ingredients to a soup that you only knew you were going to make when you saw those things in the market, hearing voices before they speak. Nothing made anything clearer to him.

"Oh!" she'd added, excited. "It's just like falling in love."

"What?" Garen had asked, still confused.

"So, you meet someone. And you don't know you're in love with them yet. And then later you are in love with them, and you realize you were the whole time and just didn't know it. And then soon after, you start to feel like you were in love with them before you ever met them, like everything before was waiting for them and everything after is learning how much you were waiting."

Garen had never been in love. When he told her this, her harshness melted away.

"I'm sorry, boy. It's just like that, though. Maybe you have to know provisioning when you see it, just like you have to know love when it happens."

Four years later Garen still didn't know love. But he knew provisioning, and much more. Yura taught him to make tinctures from herbs and roots, to sew, to garden, to cook. She taught him the name of stars he'd never really looked at before, the name of trees he passed by daily and never thought on until then. Yura became almost a mother to him, albeit more foul-mouthed than his own. She also became a guide, and his closest friend.

"Here's your wolf claw," Yura said, handing him a bundle of cloth tied with leather cord. He didn't untie it; it seemed wrong to do so here, it being so sacred for her. She handed him more things—a large leather shoulder bag, a small flat wooden chest. "Traveling supplies. You're gonna be cold where you're going, so pick up a coat. There's money in the bag, and some other stuff you'll find useful."

She unlocked the chest, opened the lid. "As many tricks I could gather for you on such short notice. You'll know what to do with 'em."

Garen scanned the vials and small pouches. Tinctures, oils, dried herbs, salves. Mostly medicines, a few cooking herbs, and...

Yura saw where his glance lingered. "Poisons."

Garen shook his head. "I'm not killing anyone."

"I'm not telling you to, boy. But the spirits say you need this, so you're taking this. Hold the key tight. I reckon they won't know what half these things are unless they've got an apothecary traveling with you. I reckon you're him, though."

Garen sat down. Emotions hit him hard, so many, so different. Loss. Fear. Excitement at his first provisioning fading into terror. Homesickness for a place he didn't call home. Humility that Yura trusted him so greatly. Gratitude for her help. Sorrow that he may never see her again.

"Yura...thank you."

The old woman hugged him, laughing. "Don't thank me. It's I who should be thanking you. Or they who should be thanking you, anyways. But you should get going, now—you have more to get before you leave. Warm clothes, like I said. And eat some."

Garen hugged her back. "Thank you, though. I mean, anyway."

She closed the chest, locked it again, and slipped it into the shoulder bag before answering. They stood together at the door now, Garen staring out into the quiet street.

"You're welcome, Garen."

Garen heard her voice tremble a bit, and politely avoided noting the sudden sadness there. He nodded, smiled and stepped into the evening.

"And one more thing," Yura called out, before closing the door behind him.

He turned, saw her smiling.

"You'll know love when you see it."

CHAPTER FIVE

The morning he was to leave, Garen woke from a dream of iron and blood into the scent of rain and his own sweat mixing with the last spectral notes of incense from the night before.

His skin and blanket were soaked; he'd fevered as he slept, wrestling against men binding him with chains and a rusting harness. He remembered the smell of mud and wet-dog, man-musk, rot, metallic taste of blood mixing with the orange-red dust of flaking iron cutting into skin.

He sat up, threw off his blankets. He expected to find pain as the fabric peeled from recent wounds, but none followed. He looked at his chest, his legs: the hair on his body was wet, matted from the sweat, but the skin underneath was whole, unscarred. His cock leaked, erect and pulsing as if he'd just a moment ago withdrawn it mid-orgasm from a man.

Garen closed his eyes, sighed, then opened them again, staring across the room at the shrine of the Lady of Provisions.

"You're gonna tell me what's happening?" he asked aloud.

No voice echoed in response.

He bathed himself quickly with cold water in a bowl. His skin was warm, hot even, but the water did not feel sharp against it. He didn't feel ill, nor even tired from the dreams. Exhilaration and heat coursed through him, like after a run, or during sex.

He'd prepared his packs the day before; nothing was left but to haul them to the western gate of the city. He dressed, pulled on his large pack, slung the second across his shoulder, turned to look one last time at his room, and left.

It was a sacred day—the streets were dead quiet. Soft morning light made the wet city feel surreal, and he a ghost or the dream of a ghost, floating upon an unfelt wind.

He didn't think: no thoughts would matter. He didn't feel: Yura had taught him early that trick. Anxiety and anticipation clouded foreseeing, colored the visions false with desire and fear. He walked, quieted, the weight of his packs pushing his feet against the ground where his own weight seemed insufficient.

He came to the gate, passed through. He walked farther, scanned the empty road. No sign of those who would come to meet him. He was not early, nor late. This was the time. These trees were the place.

There was no one.

Garen waited. Rain dripped from branches overhead onto his hood, cascaded off the waxed- leather of his packs. It was too wet to sit, but as the minutes became hours, he took off his packs and leaned against the tree.

From within the city he heard the tolling of bells marking the time. An hour passed. Another. Just after the third, he heard horses' hooves over paving stones. He looked out, caught glimpse of a group of riders. Unarmored, none wearing the uniforms of the crown or city.

He picked up his packs, walked out to meet them. The first rider rode faster when he saw Garen. His head was bare, his scalp razed. A short beard covered a muscled jaw that looked able to chew through metal.

"You're the Provisioner." It wasn't a question. The deep voice betrayed disdain.

Garen nodded.

"Where's your horse?"

The Lady hadn't told him he'd need one. Garen staved off panic, looked at the riders behind the man, then counted their horses.

"It looks like you have mine," he replied.

The man growled. "That was Veln's. He's dead. How did you know?"

Provisioning was never exact. Garen had seen nothing about horses or a dead man named Veln. He had not seen need of a horse. If he had not seen it, he would not need it.

Garen also knew it would be pointless to explain this to the man. "I knew only that I would not need a horse. I am sorry for your friend."

The man spat. "Veln was an idiot and deserved his fate."

The other riders had caught up to the first man. Garen looked across their faces, each stern, full of barely-restrained malice, but one was...*Sorn.*

Garen almost gasped in excitement, caught himself short, stared at the man's face. The man didn't stare back, showed no sign he recognized the man he'd been with the other night. When he did return Garen's gaze, it held the same bitter malevolence of the others. In fact, his face seemed suddenly so unfamiliar Garen decided he'd been mistaken. He became glad he'd said nothing.

"The Provisioner didn't bring his own horse. Give him Veln's."

The others shrugged. The man who looked like Sorn silently dismounted, unstrapped a pack from the riderless horse, put it on his own. He glanced at Garen, looking pissed, then turned to the others and said, "If the Provisioner didn't bring clothes either, then we know Thalyn's gonna die so the girl's got something to wear."

Garen's soul shrunk as the others laughed. The man's voice sounded like Sorn's; but this guy was an ass. Embarrassed he'd had any sort of emotion over him, fury welling up inside him, Garen blurted out, "I know you, right? I think I saw you praying in an alley by the docks a few weeks ago. Or kneeling, anyway."

The others laughed. The man pulled out a knife. The bearded, bald-headed man shouted. "Uric—you kill our Provisioner and you're gonna choke on that knife from inside. Let's go."

Sorn, or Uric, growled and sheathed his knife. He didn't look at Garen again. Garen felt a feeling he'd not known for years: dread of the future.

From the western gate they rode through the steady drizzling rain. The western road connected the city to no other, led instead through and upward through the forests cloaking the Istril mountains. He'd never needed to take this road, knew none of the villages they passed, recognized none of the farmland.

No one spoke. Only occasional grunts of assent or commands to the horses broke the silence. Garen tried to sense their personalities from these tiny scraps, but the men were unyielding, cold, withdrawn.

The bald, hulking, bearded man was their leader certainly, but hadn't offered his name. Garen caught it a few hours into the journey. Another rider grunted it while gesturing towards a village they glimpsed after cresting a hill.

"We stop there, Ronúr?"

Ronúr, the leader, turned his head without slowing his horse. "No, we ride to Orrunec. Veln already fucked us on time."

The others grumbled to themselves. They were wet and hungry. Garen was, too.

Just before dark, they came upon a village, twenty small houses clinging together at the edge of unruly fields. No tavern, but an elder's house. Ronúr dismounted, knocked loudly. An old woman opened the door, looked first at Ronúr, then the others. She shrugged, spoke; Ronúr barked back. Garen heard none of the words they spoke, but understood it didn't go in the woman's favor.

Ronúr then called back to the others. "Here's our lodging. Provisioner—go get us food."

"My name's Garen," he replied.

Ronúr spat back. "You don't matter, boy. You're here for what you can do. I'll slit you myself if you act like you're something else."

Garen nodded. The man's strength and rage worried him.

He dismounted, tethered the horse, and asked around the village for food to trade. The villagers were friendly once they understood he wouldn't coerce them like Ronúr. They seemed eager to keep their uninvited guests calm, and within an hour Garen had gathered enough bread, meat, cheese, and beer to feed everyone. In return he made a poultice for a woman's swollen knee, a tincture for a child who'd taken some worm in his stomach. Yura's provisions were well-seen.

Ronúr and the others stayed in the elder's house. Garen instead took the offer of the floor of an old man's home, glad to be away from the others for the night. The old man was blind and toothless; a villager brought a pot of soup for them both to eat. Garen ate with him, listened to his stories of lost loves, and of the time he and his brother set fire to the fields after eating wild mushrooms.

The man dozed; Garen put away the bowls, rinsed the pot and set it outside. As he did so, he saw through the raining night a glint of reflection from the candles inside. Someone stood a small distance from the man's house, watching him.

Garen closed the door behind him, walked out to meet the figure.

"You don't know me," came a voice as he approached. "We've never seen each other before." It was Uric. Or Sorn.

"Sure," Garen replied. "I definitely have no idea who the fuck you are, anyway."

The man look behind himself, than walked a step closer. "I'm someone who'll save your life if you don't fuck this up. Stay quiet. Don't ask questions." It was too dark to make out the man's face, but Garen imagined there was kindness there just before he turned away, walked back into the thick darkness, muttering loud enough for Garen to hear,

"Or I'll fucking kill you."

CHAPTER SIX

Garen dreamt of rust and blood again, of deep pain lanced through his shoulders and back, searing heat inside his gut, the salt taste of urine. Then cold, metal taste of snow, dull ache of broken bone, scent of burning pine. Old stone, eyes staring through smoke, sound of weeping and a voice in reply.

"Do it, please." Words tortured but kind. A woman on a threshold, before childbirth or death.

A man crying. *"I love you."* Then a blade, bone, muscle, and tendon severed. Heaviness, a river unleashed, a day ended, the last quake of orgasm, shallow breath. A yelping cry. Sleep, then a crash of wood.

Garen woke, blinked into the flood of morning light, stared at a broken door and the man who'd broken it, Thalyn. His face sneered, but he looked unwell, or unslept.

"Get up. We leave now."

He still heard the weeping of the man in his dream, smelled wood smoke, but felt no pain, only sorrow. Thalyn had not waited for an answer, was already gone.

He looked at the damage to the door again, then to the old man still sleeping. Garen stood, rolled and tied his blankets, then placed a coin upon the small table so his host would wake to more than a guest gone and a broken door.

The morning was grey, wet; the air uneasy. He heard low voices, the horses unquiet, shaking their tack, then saw the men gathered outside the elder's house. Villagers were there, too, a short distance away, staring at a heap of clothing near the men.

Garen gasped when he could see better. The elder was dead, her blood puddling in the mud. Ronúr, Sorn, and two of the others were already on their horses; Thalyn was just mounting his. They eyed the villagers, the villagers glared in return.

"What happened?" Garen called, drawing their attention on him.

"The wench tried to hex us," Ronúr growled. "Get on your horse before I have to kill the rest of them."

The villagers remained silent, stared at Garen. He caught the face of the woman whose child he helped. A sense passed from her gaze to his, a pleading urgency. *Make them leave,* he heard, though not from her lips.

Garen strode faster to his horse, tried to read Sorn's face as he mounted. Jaw set, eyes unblinking, a dead stare into the distance beyond their leader. He couldn't catch his attention, nor did he know what he'd hope to come after it.

Ronúr ordered his horse on with a hard gait; the others fol- lowed. Garen had only ever ridden pack horses, never at a gallop. He held fast, tried not to yank the horse's bit. He turned his own head long enough to see the crowd had moved to the dead woman's body, heard weeping, then set his eyes on the road before them.

They rode like this for what seemed an hour, as if chased. Garen had seen no horses in the village besides their own; none could have come to take revenge. Ronúr was himself strong enough to take on several of them, even without arms: they had no reason for fear. Still, Ronúr led the pace as if they were in danger.

The road began to incline. Farmland swelling under autumn fullness gave way to reddening forests of birch, alder, oak and pine. Ronúr signed for them to slow when the ruins of a tower came into view. When they reached it he allowed them to stop to rest the horses and to eat.

Garen dismounted last, inclining his ears for word of what had brought the old woman's death. No one spoke of it; after they tethered their horses to trees they sat and ate, wordless. Ronúr and Thalyn sat together, Sorn and the other two kept their own company apart.

Garen watched the others while he washed down dry bread and hard cheese with water. The rain had stopped; enough sun flowed through the sky that he took off his coat and overshirt. The sun warmed his skin. This eased him.

He stood and walked to the tower. A little taller than the trees around it, eight men high he guessed. Part of its wall a wreck of tumbled-down stone, a rusted-iron door barricaded with bramble. Ivy as thick as oak branches climbed the rest of the tower's height: he guessed it hadn't been used for decades, maybe centuries.

"It's from before Verych." One of the other men, whose name he hadn't yet caught, had followed him.

It was older than Garen had guessed. Verych was founded over six-hundred years ago. Garen turned to the man. "I guess it's in good shape, then."

"Plague. They barred themselves in to escape it. Didn't help them, or any of the others. Lots more of them where we're going."

Garen straightened, relieved finally to learn anything about their journey. "What's your name?"

"Huvwn. Your riding my brother's horse."

Huvwn's face—straight brow, narrow dark eyes, mouth obscured by a short black beard— betrayed no emotion. Garen stayed silent rather than try to respond.

"He was an idiot."

"That's what Ronúr said, too. What happened?"

Huvwn spat. "Thought he'd have a last night of whoring. Found him in his bed with his chest split clean open."

The man's calm voice unnerved Garen. "Who killed him?"

Huvwn jerked his head slightly behind them. "Thalyn, probably. Or maybe men from Arras. Fucked either way."

Garen's mind felt slow, sluggish. Arras was the enemy against whom everyone in the city was clamoring for war; if they killed Veln, that meant Garen's companions were closer to the king of Verych than he suspected. But if Thalyn had killed Veln, then why was Huvwn so calm?

He couldn't sort it, so he changed the subject. "What did the elder do to Ronúr?"

Huvwn shook his head. "Nothing, probably." Then glancing behind them, he muttered "Ronúr's a paranoid fool. Terrified of anything wyrd. That's why he hates you."

Garen nodded. "What's the other guy's name?"

"Which other? Uric? Or Jord?"

Huvwn didn't know Uric had another identity, then. "I meant Jord." Then realising Huvwn might tell him more about Sorn, he added, "but neither of them speak much, huh?"

"Both are Ronúr's men along with Thalyn, but Thalyn is Ronúr's *man*, if you understand me. Jord only talks in his sleep. Crazy talk, too, stuff about killing kids. But Uric's the one you need to stay away from. Watched him gut an old priest for insulting Ronúr. Ripped his stomach open with the handle of a bell, pulled his entrails out, and then gods-damned shoved them in the priest's mouth. Don't piss him off."

Garen tried not to blanch, but was certain he looked ill. "So you and Veln weren't Ronúr's men?"

Thalyn's voice reached their ears, not very far away. Huvwn shook his head. "Just started working for him last year." Then, he whispered, "sorry."

Before Garen could ask "for what?" Huvwn pushed him hard. He fell backwards, landing in the brambles, thorns lacerating his arms, legs, and face. He cut himself more as he tried to struggle free, then stopped long enough to hear Huvwn's response to laughter behind them.

Garen could only barely see the man who'd laughed. It was Thalyn. Huwvn spoke to him. "I told you the boy's harmless. He had nothing to do with Veln. Tell Ronúr to stop worrying.

He only listens to you."

Thalyn walked past Huvwn, glaring down at Garen's battle with the briars. Garen returned his gaze, indignant. Thalyn said nothing, appeared suddenly unnerved, then turned and walked with Huvwn back towards the others.

Blood dripped into his eye from a gouge in his forehead. The pain everywhere was awful, dozens of tiny stab-wounds everywhere on his body, but the humiliation felt even worse. "You didn't show me this," he growled, angrily, at the air. "None of this." He pulled one vine away, another snapped back into his face.

"Yura was right," he cursed, then felt even worse for it.

But then maybe his teacher wasn't completely wrong. In just the last week he'd waken in stables next to a man he didn't remember; that man threatened him last night and apparently murdered priests. Last night he'd settled with a group of strange men into a village for the night; this morning the leader of those men had killed an old woman. And now he was covered in scratches and blood after another one of those men threw him into brambles.

Yura didn't trust She-Who-Foresees, never thought Her help was worth the cost. Only a few days ago, the idea of a balance sheet between what She gave and what She demanded had seen profane to Garen; now, he wondered if he'd never respected himself enough to notice what he'd put out. Maybe it all wasn't worth it. Or maybe he'd never really thought that he was.

Being alone with these thoughts terrified Garen. Yura was far away, as were his remaining few friends. Garen shook his head: he hadn't even told them he was leaving the city. Perhaps they wouldn't even have noticed. Perhaps they weren't really even his friends at all.

He stared at his bloodied arms and hands, trying to find there something to make sense of the awful ache he suddenly felt inside him. Worse, it was not so sudden—slowly and with panicked fear he understood it was an ache he'd always felt but never until now dared name.

He was *alone.*

There was no one who understood him, no one he understood. He was outside the world, outside all human meaning, clinging desperately to his faith in an unseen goddess who'd never really lifted him from the edge of this abyss of loneliness, only ever kept him from plummeting into it.

Anger became terror, terror became despair, and despair became resignation. He trudged back to the rest of the men, biting back the razor-pain of the scratches, not bothering to clean the blood from his face. To any other group of people he might have looked a thing of horror or pity. For these men, however, the gouges in his skin and blood clotting on his face was hilarious. Ronúr sneered, Thalyn laughed, Huvwn and Jord shared a conspiratorial joke between them.

Garen met each of their gazes with a calm rage. He had nothing to lose; he was already alone, doubting even the final thread that tied him to meaning. They couldn't harm him further. He saved the greatest anger for Sorn, or Uric, or whomever he really was. But when he turned to look at him, he found something else.

Sorn wasn't laughing at all. His face looked kind, almost sympathetic, and a little angry himself.

CHAPTER SEVEN

The men didn't speak beyond that as they continued their ride. Garen was glad of this: he had nothing to say to them, and even less he wanted to hear. His curiosity had waned, replaced with growing anger and resentment towards them all, even— and perhaps most of all—Sorn. Or Uric. Or whomever he really was.

Garen stayed sullen, watching the landscape pass by him. Occasionally he'd see other ruins: more towers, the remnants of mills, stone walls overthrown by tree roots, cottages of long-dead farmers with long-missing roofs, old shrines atop choked fountains whose spirits no longer had statues. An entire village empty of life, then another, half-submerged by a lake from an overflowed mining dam.

Nothing felt fully desolate about this emptiness, however. No humans but themselves, yet the forsaken houses felt alive nevertheless with what lives best when no one's around to stop it. Meadows dotted with unrestrained trees and wilding grains mixed with native grasses and flowers; remnants of an orchard still bearing pears and hazelnuts where ravens kept their raucous councils, swarms of bees from forgotten apiaries no longer worried by their thieving keepers. Life expanding in the absence of other life, multiplying now that no human could keep the fences secure and the streams channeled.

Not until they stopped for the evening did Garen begin to question precisely why everything had been abandoned. Since the village of Orrunec they had seen no sign of habitation, but the old imperial stone roads they followed were still in decent repair. Someone still traveled this way—perhaps not recently, but enough to keep nature from overtaking the paths.

They set up camp in a series of stone buildings that looked once to have been held by merchants. The wall around the courtyard was still intact, as were the roofs of several of the houses; the water in the pump-house was good, not stagnant, and the chimney of the main hearth wasn't blocked.

Garen quickly realized his role was to be not just Provisioner but also camp cook and servant for the other men. And as no-one offered to help, he spent the first hour of their arrival gathering wood and water to cook with. This made Garen more angry and loath to speak, but his curiosity had returned. This villa appeared only recently abandoned, and hadn't been stripped of its possessions neither then nor after: he found a moth-eaten fur jerkin in one room, unopened wine bottles (which the others quickly claimed), dusty and rotting bed clothes, and even a few unpillaged heavily-tarnished silver plates.

The stew he made for the men put them in an almost jovial, talking humor, aided in no small part by some of the "spices" Garen added from the collection Yura had prepared for him.

So after dinner, he set aside his anger and asked aloud why so much here had been abandoned, and when.

The others ignored his question, but Huwvn barked an answer. "Plague came back. Ain't that right, Ronúr?"

Ronúr grunted. "That's what they get. Should have spread to Orrunec, too."

Garen noted something pass between Huwvn and Ronúr that he couldn't quite read. Some other level of meaning he couldn't catch, with a sharp note of restrained anger from the leader. Jord and Uric merely continued eating, but Garen saw a brief, unreadable glance pass between Ronúr and Thalyn which made him decide not to press the matter further.

After dinner, the other men set themselves up for sleep in the main house, but after washing up and making sure the fire would be strong enough for the rest of the night, he brought his pack into a smaller house nearby, probably a servant's quarters. Here he could be alone for awhile, away from the others and their attention. Seclusion was what he needed most; what he needed most to do could not be done without it.

He didn't wait until he'd unpacked his bedroll onto the floor, nor any of the other things he knew he really ought to have done. Instead, he pulled out a small wooden box, unlocked it, and spread its contents across the dust-covered stone table he'd chosen the room for.

A few moments of fumbling with flint against steel and the tinder lit, from which he pulled flame to light a candle and crumbling charcoal. A crystal of sticky resin upon the coal, he whispered: "Lady of the stars, Lady of the grave."

He daubed mandrake oil on his forehead and the back of his neck. "Lady of the future, Lady of the past." Inhaling the incense deeply, he stared through the smoke at Her image, and then chanted, "Lady of our darkness, Lady of our light."

And then Garen sat, mute, his mind empty, his other eyes searching, his other ears listening.

When Yura first taught him to See-as-She-Sees, she'd warned him he'd understand nothing. Yura, as with too much else, was quite correct. Garen rarely tried this ritual any longer, each previous attempt driving him to moments of near madness. Everything was always fragments and too fast, as if someone had cut several paintings he'd never seen before into tiny pieces and laid them scattered before him saying, "hurry —put these back together."

It had seemed a useless ritual, except only once. He'd rarely ever let himself out for hire, both unsure of his own abilities and fearful of drawing too much attention to himself. But once a woman asked him find her missing child, and her obvious pain had moved him enough to try. That time, he'd performed the ritual of sight and the pieces felt bigger, almost complete in themselves.

He'd stared at the fragments, listened to the scattered and un-patterned voices and found suddenly a pattern. As with throwing bones or the sortilege of leaves, he'd understood you didn't have to look at everything you were shown, only the parts that told the story you needed to know. But that time, the story of her child's fate had horrified him too much to tell it all true to the woman, and instead he merely let her know her child had died.

Garen thought he'd never use the ritual again after that, but here they were again, the flood of images, the riotous movements, the cacophony of voices. Too much to make sense of, too much to understand. *"Only the story I need,"* he whispered to himself, and tried to sort the visions.

He saw people in rags kneeling in snow, children screaming. An old woman's sing-song prayers at a shrine of bird bones, rising to fever-pitch. Eyes staring from a forest. A symbol carved with blackened metal into the chest of a writhing man. Blood on snow, more blood on snow, blood upon wooden planks, blood smeared across the bark of a tree.

"What are you doing boy?"

Garen reeled from the visions, shook himself into this-world and the voice which had interrupted the ritual. It was Uric again, or Sorn.

"Provisioning," he answered from somewhere in his throat.

The man who was Uric and Sorn didn't move from the doorway where he'd stood, watching. "What did you see?"

Garen was too tired to give a more cryptic answer. "Nothing I can make sense of yet. But I guess Ronúr was right—the elder did try to hex him."

The man made a series of quick movements, shutting the door behind himself, crouching suddenly next to Garen. "Don't tell him that, or Thalyn."

Garen didn't shrink from his presence. "Why would I? And what's your real name?"

The man grunted. "I'm who I say I am. Call me anything else but Uric and you'll never speak again."

Garen shrugged, ignoring the threat. "It was you that night. I don't care for whatever game you're playing here, but I won't reveal your hand. For all your talk, you're the only one who doesn't seem to want me dead."

Uric grunted. "Everyone wants everyone else dead here. When we find our prey, more than likely half of us won't make it back alive for the ransom."

He seized on this hint. "What prey? What ransom? I don't know why I'm here."

A subtle note of sympathy tinged Uric's response. "You really don't know? We're wolf-hunting."

Garen almost laughed, then suddenly remembered the paw. "But all the wolves are dead."

"One was spotted last year. The king wants it for a trophy, they say."

All this effort—and the conscription of a Provisioner —seemed all a bit too much for one animal. "Then why am I here?"

Uric shrugged. "You know as much as I do. I'm just muscle here."

Despite what felt like a comfortable ease with him, Huwvn's story about Uric suddenly re- appeared in Garen's mind. "Is it true you killed a priest?"

"Why wouldn't it be?"

This answer didn't sit well. "Because I'm having a hard time imagining the guy in those stables killing anyone."

Uric's hand suddenly gripped Garen's neck, paralyzing him. "I should kill you just for mentioning that."

Terror mixed with an unwelcome sense of arousal. It indeed felt Uric could kill him, but also that he might just as easily kiss him. But neither happened, and Uric released his grip.

Blood rushed burning to Garen's head. "Then why not, mate? You too coward to kill me or too coward to be known for loving men?"

Uric spat. "I love no one. You were a good lay, that's why you're still alive. Don't push it."

Garen didn't answer. The fear sharpened his desire, and he tried to push both of those feelings as far away as he could.

Uric said nothing more for a few heavy breaths, than continued. "There's more here than you think, more than I think. You said it's strange they needed a Provisioner to hunt an animal. You're right—everyone else thinks so too. Everyone but Ronúr, who isn't even telling Thalyn what's really happening here."

"Huwvn said Thalyn's closest to Ronúr..."

Uric laughed. "Thalyn's his lover, and a paranoid prat. Ronúr takes whatever piece of meat he wants, man or woman, as long as it's alive. So if Thalyn thinks you're in Ronúr's sights, he'll kill you before Ronúr's had a chance to taste you."

"Ah," Garen said. "So Thalyn killed Huwvn's brother?"

"That's what they all believe, yeah."

Garen traced a hidden meaning in Uric's words. "You don't believe it..."

Uric shrugged. "If you'd've seen Veln's body, you'd guess it was someone a lot more brutal than Thalyn."

"Oh," Garen answered, backing away slowly. "You killed him."

Uric's voice betrayed no remorse. "You're not complaining, are you? I mean, you got a horse out of it."

Nothing felt safe any longer, and Garen suddenly hated how

much he still lusted after the killer in front of him. "You're scaring me. But I guess you know that."

Uric nodded. "Good. Now that I have your attention, I need you to listen to everything I tell you from here on out. You'll speak nothing of this to others, and you'll let me know if you find out what's in that wooden chest Ronúr carries with him everywhere."

Garen had seen the chest, yes. Long and narrow, covered in leather, apparently heavy from the way even Ronúr's heavily-muscled arms hefted it. He'd thought nothing of the thing, assumed it to be full of crossbow bolts or heavy swords, maybe silver. It hadn't drawn his attention beyond that, but now that Uric mentioned it, Garen recalled finding it odd Ronúr never parted from the thing.

"What do you think is in there?" Garen asked, glad to be talking of something else besides murder.

"It doesn't matter what I think. I need to know. Whatever it is, its key to what we're really up here for."

So maybe Uric didn't believe they were really hunting a wolf. Garen didn't press further, didn't see the point. He wanted to be left alone, not to return to his ritual but to hide from the entire absurd situation. Uric seemed to comply, stood up. But before he turned to leave, his vise grip was on the Garen's neck again, this time pulling him for a kiss from which Garen didn't have the will to struggle against.

"Your throat's better than most," Uric grunted, then suddenly pulled away.

Garen struggled against the trembling heat of his own body. "I don't—I don't remember everything that happened."

Uric grunted. "I'll make you remember next time. Not—not here." And he turned to walk away, but Garen wasn't ready to let him leave so quickly.

"I don't even remember meeting. What happened? Did you know I was a Provisioner?"

Uric stopped at the door but didn't turn around. "No. The minute I saw that you were the one they divined for this I thought it was a shame I'd probably have to kill you too. Don't fuck up and I won't have to."

Garen watched him leave into the dark courtyard, and sighed.

CHAPTER EIGHT

Despite having been shaken from his conversation with Uric and the confused images from the ritual, Garen had managed to sleep deeply and dreamlessly. Autumnal early morning light streamed through the dust-covered windows, illuminating all in a soft, calm yellow not too much different from late summer evenings.

He lingered a bit on his bedroll, holding onto to the warmth which still lingered there. The air was crisp but not too chill, a faint smell of incense from last night's ritual still hanging like recent memory.

Garen thought on the images again. The chanting woman had been the elder of the village, certainly. She'd tried to hex Ronúr and perhaps the others, but the words she'd used were not those of vengeance but rather prevention. Misdirection, actually—the bird bones were probably a shrine to one of the many traveling spirits, popular with vagabonds, nomads, refugees, and smugglers. Garen couldn't summon to memory the specific words she'd used, only their sense. But that sense was clear: she'd begged the spirit to confound the men on their journey.

So she had sensed something of their goal, or perhaps overheard some talk of it between Ronúr and Thalyn. Either way, she'd sought to misdirect them, prevent them from finding their prey. And that act ended her life when Ronúr discovered it.

Garen shook his head in wonder at his slowness. The bones were those of carrion crows: the ritual hadn't resulted in her death, but rather *required* it. The specific spirit she'd asked was one no one built shrines for anymore, but was popular during the years of plague. It inhabited the dead as they rotted, lived in decomposition, consumed failed dreams to turn lost causes into unexpected hope.

The elder hadn't been so old to be near death, though, and she must have known the men would only stay one night. Even the most vindictive of people would never call on Ul'dre'na to hex someone in such circumstances. She must have foreseen something, then, something Garen couldn't see. Her own life had been less important to her than stopping them from what they intended to do.

But what were they doing? Hunting an extinct wolf, apparently. Uric didn't appear to really believe that, perhaps the others didn't either. The answer was probably in that chest Ronúr carried, but Garen had no hopes of getting near it without being noticed.

Garen turned to the other images. The people kneeling in snow, and then all the blood. Those, he thought, were probably the people who once lived in these abandoned villages. They'd not died of plague, but rather the plague of swords:

they were killed. Plague victims would have left corpses, or at least bones picked clean by bird, rodent, and worm. They'd seen nothing of the sort on the road, nor here in this villa, and Garen suspected they'd see none further into the mountains, either.

So that had been that look between Huwvn and Ronúr. It wasn't plague, and they both knew otherwise. And when Ronúr had said it "should have spread to Orrunec, too," he'd meant those villagers should have been killed as well.

Perhaps they'd been around for the killings. *Perhaps they had been the ones doing the killing.*

Recalling the villages he'd seen with his eyes and the deaths he'd seen with his other eyes, he understood: the people in these mountains had not just been killed, but rather punished and purged. Orrunec was the first inhabited village coming down from these mountains; the people there were spared, but must have known what happened to the others. So too the elder, who'd sacrificed herself to prevent more killing. Whether or not her ritual worked, Garen couldn't know yet. Perhaps he was under the same spell as the other men, or perhaps he would become unwitting agent to the contracted spirit.

Garen rose, shook out his bedroll and tied it to his pack. The rest of the images were too obscure for him to understand, but he we was certain he didn't like where they were probably pointing.

Relieving himself against a knotted pine whose roots pushed up part of the sandstone paving stones in the villa, Garen then washed his face and drank from a small spring in what was once a terraced garden. The spring was sacred, but there was now no statue or offerings in the votive alcove above its mouth. The water tasted sharp, with the metal taste of cold snow-melt. Likely some mineral quality benefited the drinker, but which mineral he could not guess. Garen muttered a brief greeting to it.

Now more awake, his mind feeling more clear, he crossed the courtyard of the villa to the larger manse where the others had slept. He heard stirrings; a few had wakened already, and he guessed they'd be demanding breakfast soon enough. At this idea he sighed; he had no desire to tend to them, let alone even be with them any longer.

Before entering he let his eyes wander into the forested hills surrounding them. He couldn't, of course, but the idea of merely walking into them, away from all this, suddenly thrilled them. He'd not survive long: not enough food for more than a few days, no real sense of where he even was or how to survive. His skills were useful in cities, or with others, but Garen didn't suspect they'd be of use so far from civilization.

He sighed, and entered, finding Huwvn and Jord drinking from their flasks in front of a re- stoked hearth fire. They at least could do that for himself, Garen mused, then shook his head at the wrong turn in his thinking. Of course they could do that for themselves. They could do all of it, and merely wanted a servant to save them the effort.

"'Bout time you woke, boy," Huwyn grunted. "Where's our breakfast?"

Garen bit his tongue. "On it. Was checking the fire."

Jord threw a large log into the hearth forcefully, sending embers bursting in a cloud around him. "We got it. Do your work."

Jord looked either too drunk or too tired to notice the embers that had landed on his leather trousers. For a moment Garen considered telling him, then shrugged and left. He walked slowly across the courtyard to where they'd stabled their horses, straining a bit to hear Jord's inevitable shout of anger. He wasn't disappointed.

But another matter pushed all that immediately out of his head. Training his attention on the manse at the expense of everything else around him, he'd not noticed the silence from within the stables until after he opened the door.

It was then he saw the horses, silent, crumpled upon the ground. Dead.

Garen shouted back towards the men in the manse as he entered the stables. All six horses lay on the wooden floor, some of their legs splayed out like branches, others contorted under their bodies as they'd fallen. He went to the closest horse, the one Ronúr had been riding. A black ichor, too dark to be only blood, caked around its still-open eyes and nostrils.

He stepped back, shaking, just at the moment that Huwvyn and Jord bolted in behind him. "Fuck's sake, man. What the?"

Garen turned and saw the two men as shocked as he'd been. Huwvyn barked at Jord to get Ronúr, who complied after muttering something under his breath that sounded like the word, "ghosts." Garen pointed to the black stuff around the horse's face, but Huwyn ignored him.

"Ronúr's going to kill you, boy."

The words shocked Garen even more than the dead horses had. "Wait—why me? I didn't do this."

"You're a Provisioner. You should have seen that this would happen."

Garen shrunk inside himself at the words. "That's...that's not how this works!"

Huwyn had pulled a knife from his belt and held it suddenly close to Garen's chest. "You see the future, and you didn't see this. Maybe you're not even a Provisioner after all. You might be..."

"He's not," came another voice, just as suddenly. It was Uric, shirtless, still belting his trousers from sleep. He'd heard Garen's shout when the others had, then.

"Fuck all you know, Uric," Huwyn spat. "Look at the horses."

And Uric did, stooping to stare at their faces like Garen had. "Put down your knife, Huwvn. Ronúr was right."

And just at that moment, Ronúr growled back from the courtyard. "Right about what?"

Uric stood upright. He looked at Huwvyn, still holding the knife towards Garen, then grabbed it from his hand and threw it on the ground. Then he walked past both of them towards the door of the stables.

"The horses are dead, Ronúr. Some plague, it looks like. You were right to kill that witch."

Ronúr strode in past Uric, pushed Huwvyn and Garen out of his way, then kicked his dead horse. "That wench!" he shouted, then kicked another horse.

Garen could only cower at Ronúr's rage. Worse, just then Huwvyn started in again. "This Provisioner is shit," he said, pointing at Garen. "Should have seen this."

Ronúr grunted, and for a brief moment Garen felt a fleeting admiration for the man. "We don't need them from here. Path gets too hard for them after the abbey anyway. Was thinking of leaving them there, but looks like here's as good a place as any."

Garen suddenly liked Ronúr, and for the first time really took in the man's presence. Like Uric he was shirtless, and Garen stared a bit in awe at the inked and scarred skin pulled tight against Ronúr's muscled chest. He was terrifying, but also attractive in a brutal, dangerous way.

The moment passed quickly, though, as Garen hit upon the same flaw in Ronúr's logic as Huwvyn countered, "we'll need them to get back, though."

Garen saw something pass across Ronúr's face that made him very uneasy. He seemed about to say something else, something Garen thought he could hear in his memory, something he didn't want to hear. But instead, Ronúr grunted again and said only, "we'll walk."

And then he strode out, and Huwvn and Jord followed him. Garen was still shaking, hadn't really tried to linger behind with Uric, but also hadn't been in a hurry to return to the manse. Uric hadn't been in a hurry either, and so there they both were, alone for a moment in a stable full of dead horses.

"Thank you," Garen whispered quietly.

"I didn't do anything. And anyway, I want to know why you didn't see this."

Garen began to protest. "You heard me. That's now how this works. I only see what I need to see, and like Ronúr said, we probably don't need the horses."

Uric clenched his teeth, staring hard into Garen's eyes. "You don't get it, huh? Why do you think we don't need horses? How's Ronúr gonna chase down a wolf without a horse? And how's he gonna haul it back down the mountain on foot?"

"He'll make us carry it, probably?" Garen tried, not understanding so much why this mattered.

"You're an idiot, Garen. Listen to me." He lowered his voice. "Ronúr took that all like it was nothing. That's not him—he's quicker to rage than anyone I've met. So he wasn't expecting the horses on the way back down either. We're missing something."

Uric's conspiratorial tone felt strangely intimate to Garen. Or maybe it was that Uric had said, "we." Either way, what Uric was saying made some sense—Ronúr did seem oddly calm considering the circumstances. And what had it been that Garen thought he was going to say instead?

Boot steps echoing off the stone in the courtyard made them both drop the subject. It was Thalyn now, the last one to see the horses. But when he got to the door he showed no interest in the carnage.

He look distractedly at Garen as he said, "we move after breakfast. Get going on it." And then speaking to Uric, an unmistakable note of malice toning each word. "Your pack is outside the stables—you're scout today. Wait for us at the abbey."

Garen hoped that Thalyn would leave them, but instead he waited for them to walk ahead of him. He wanted more than anything to ask why Uric's face was suddenly lined with something that looked like both malice and victory.

CHAPTER NINE

Garen fed them coffee and boiled oats mixed with part of the bacon he'd traded for in Orrunec. No one was happy about the meal, but he spat back that provisioning didn't mean providing for everyone's preferences, just making sure they were fed.

He was surprised at himself for saying this so forcefully to them, and even more surprised their response was merely to grumble and eat more. He was in a foul mood, a mood made more foul by Uric's sudden absence. As frustrating—and constantly frightening—as Uric had been for Garen, he was the only one he felt he could almost trust.

No. It was worse than that. The feeling that passed through Garen when he understood Uric would be elsewhere was more a sharp ache in his gut rather than a mere sense of disappointment. He tried to put this thought out of his head and feeling out of his stomach. Neither would easily leave. He couldn't possibly be feeling this way for a man who'd lied to him, who'd threaten to kill him multiple times, and who evidently had a history of making good on such threats.

No. He *could*, he thought. But that wasn't the right question. Not *"could he,"* but rather *"should he?"* And there, Garen was quite certain of the answer. No, he should not. Not at all.

It was while struggling with this absurd thought that Garen suddenly noticed the men around him had gone alarmingly silent. They'd all been eating, complaining about things or trading sharp jabs at each other, but now they weren't. No one was making a sound.

He looked from his bowl to see they were all staring at him.

"Answer the question." It was Ronúr speaking, and he was speaking to him.

He hadn't heard it. He looked at the others, hoping to find some clue to what he'd missed. The expressions on their faces were blank, expectant, except for Thalyn's. Thalyn looked furious, and also scared, like a cornered animal.

"I–" Garen started, but was saved by Ronúr's temper.

"Answer me," he barked again. "Did Thalyn tell Uric I ordered him ahead?"

An easy question, then. "Yeah. He said–"

But before he could finish, he was throwing himself out of the way from the two men as quickly as the others were, because Ronúr was on top of Thalyn, beating him repeatedly with his fists. No one tried to intervene, nor had the idea even occurred to Garen: Ronúr's rage was as terrible as his strength. Over and over he punched Thalyn, mostly in the face, a few times in the side, and even the distance Garen had managed to put between himself and the fight wasn't far enough away to keep Thalyn's blood splattering on him.

As much as he wanted to flee what was happening, he found himself transfixed on the violence. He couldn't look away, or didn't really want to. No one else looked away either, until it was done. Ronúr stood up, his hands and chest slick with blood, and spoke again to Garen.

"Fix him up," he said, with a dismissive gesture towards Thalyn. And then he went outside to wash himself at the pumphouse.

Jord and Huwvyn didn't speak, but they also didn't look at Thalyn. Garen didn't really want to look at him, either, but he needed to if he were to "fix" him. So he stood up, took a few steps, and regarded the pulp of a man Thalyn had become.

It was bad, or was probably bad under all the gore. He couldn't see much for the blood, except that one of Thalyn's eyes were already swollen shut. And several teeth laid in the darkening pool of blood next to his face, probably explaining much of what was coming from his mouth.

"Damn," Garen said, trying to seem calm. "I'll need some hot water." And then, noticing neither Huwvyn nor Jord moved when he said this, he sighed. "So...I'll boil some, I guess."

He took a small pot with him into the courtyard, where Ronúr was still washing off Thalyn's blood. Garen didn't really want to approach him, but standing there watching him dumbly wasn't an option either. So he crossed the yard to the small servant's house, grabbed Yura's apothecary chest from his pack, and set out back towards the well.

Ronúr had finished, but he hadn't left. Water dripped from his face, from his beard, from his chest. His scars looked more severe like this, his tattoos angrier, his muscles more like stone than mere flesh.

Garen met his eyes as he approached the fountain. Ronúr was staring at him, unblinking. Garen didn't want to hold his gaze, wanted to look away, but something in him revolted against this act of submission.

He said nothing as he held the pot under the stream. Ronúr hadn't moved to make space for him, so Garen had to hold the pot with his arm stretched at full length, an awkward position. It also brought Garen much closer to Ronúr than he wanted to be.

It felt like an eternity, waiting for the pot to fill, standing so close to him. Garen could hear Ronúr's breath over the sound of the water, almost feel his breath. And still Ronúr didn't move, said nothing until finally grunting, "he'll live."

"Yes," Garen replied back, trying to keep his voice even. "I can't do anything for his teeth though."

Garen hadn't meant that as an accusation, but Ronúr's sudden choking grip around his neck meant he'd take it that way regardless.

"He made me do it."

Despite the pain and panic of Ronúr crushing his throat, Garen almost laughed. Ronúr sounded ridiculous, like a petulant child trying to avoid punishment for hitting a sibling. Suddenly all the scars on his chest, the brusqueness of his personality, and the strength of his muscles seemed like a bad joke.

Garen, still managing to hold the pot of water, resisted the urge to mock the man and instead tried to nod. Ronúr released his grip, let Garen go, and stood wordlessly. Garen met his eyes, saw something terrifying and yet also terrified in the man's expression, then carried the water and the apothecary chest back to the house.

Thalyn hadn't moved, nor had the others moved him, nor had they even remained in the hearth room. Whether because they disliked Thalyn or feared Ronúr's wrath Garen didn't know or even care. He was finding the whole lot of them rather pathetic.

While he waited for the water to boil, Garen tore one of his shirts into shreds and began cleaning off some of the blood on Thalyn's face. He was unconscious, which helped Garen get the blood off faster. His eye had swollen even more in the few minutes Garen had been away, and his nose was quite broken. Opening his mouth wider he found another broken tooth, for-tunately unswallowed.

Garen turned Thalyn's head slightly, feeling behind it for a wound. He found one—no doubt from falling on the stone floor, but it wasn't too deep. Then he opened Thalyn's shirt. There was an expansive purple bruise on the right side of his chest, A rib or two was probably cracked, but nothing pro-truded. From this and the sound of Thalyn's breathing, Garen assumed his lungs hadn't been punctured.

He rinsed the cloth and then his hands in the colder water he'd reserved from boiling, dried his hands on his trousers, and then opened the chest with the key he kept suspended from a small cord around his neck.

Yura had provisioned him very, very well. Scores of tinctures, extracts, waters, oils, and powders from every plant and stone he could ever require, each in slim corked bottles labeled with her minuscule lettering. There was enough there to cure any ailment he could think of, and probably quite a few more he'd never encountered.

Studying healing with her had been his favorite part of learning to be a Provisioner, and also she'd said the most important. Provisioners were only begrudgingly accepted in the empire, and at times previous had been even less accepted and more persecuted. "Healing's how we kept alive," she'd explained, recounting how when they were forbidden to practice provisioning they were still sought out—even by lords and antagonistic priests—for their ability to cure.

"Especially the unmentionable problems, which is why I'm teaching 'em first." By "unmentionable" she'd meant all the rashes, the spotting, the warting and the foul odors and the pusses that spread through carnal joy, and the most unmentionable of all, the pregnancies.

And so he had learned with her how make the body revolt against the seed of a man with tisanes and tinctures. And also how to make piss flow clear and clean again with dried berries and powdered roots, to clear the burning in the throat or the itching on the cock or the cunt or the ass, to burn away warts and to stop the weeping wounds. He learned all this before the other ailments, listening awkwardly to each story Yura recounted about those she treated. Yura never seemed able to teach without an accompanying narrative, and some of the tales were quite lurid.

But by the end, he knew not only how to heal the problems of sex and to poison the body to stop a pregnancy, but also how to heal most other things. Core to all this was how to find illness in the first place, and here Yura would constantly remind him how Provisioners would always be superior to the learned doctors. "We're cheating and I don't care," she laughed. "They have to study and guess, we just know what's wrong."

"We have to study too," Garen had replied. "I mean, you're teaching me what to do."

"But you'll know what's wrong when you look at someone. They don't. They have to guess, and then they poison the sick person, who gets more sick and sometimes too sick for me to help. Like this one time, this woman comes to me and she's blind, but she wasn't blind when she'd paid a doctor to make her moon-bleed not hurt so much. And so she was blind and bleeding even more than usual. Died a week later. Nothing I could do."

Yura had showed him how to feel the body of a person —even without touching it and sometimes without even seeing it—to know what was wrong. With Thalyn it was much easier than others, as he already knew what was wrong with him. He'd been beaten up, hit repeatedly by Ronúr. There wasn't much else to know and really not much to do, either. He'd have to clean the wounds, burn away any possible infection, and sew the skin together. The bruises and the cracked ribs would need some bone-mend herbs, his swollen eye would need some ice-wort and maybe a slight puncture to release the fluid. And as he'd told Ronúr, there was nothing he could do about Thalyn's teeth.

Garen started to pull out the vials he'd need, then felt a chill shock. Some of the other vials were empty. They weren't necessary for what he did, but he was certain they'd been full when last he opened the box. He read the labels: black wort, clot-bane, potter's hat. Each were empty, each had been full. Yura had provided him enough herbs in those vials to kill a horse.

Or *six horses*, he understood suddenly with horror.

He thought again on the black ichor issuing from their eyes and nostrils. Small amounts of clot-bane would keep a heart from stopping, but with potter's hat the heart would have sped to bursting while blackwort dissolved all the soft tissue in the body.

I did this, he thought. No one else could have; he had the only key to the apothecary chest, and it couldn't have been opened without it. It was a puzzle box: the keyhole wouldn't even accept the key without a series of seamless panels being depressed first.

So he let drop his one vain hope that maybe Uric had stolen the key from him while he slept. Unless he was also a Provisioner, he wouldn't even have known that combination of poisons. And whoever Uric or Sorn actually was, Garen was certain he was not a Provisioner.

Garen had killed the horses, then. While he slept, or while he thought he slept. As had happened to him so many times before, and also to Yura, She-Who-Foresees had sent him off, unconscious, in the middle of the night. And this time it was to kill horses.

He shook his head. The black ichor in their eyes and nostrils made them look to have died from plague. No, this wasn't Her. This was Ul'dre'na, the spirit called by the elder Ronúr murdered. Likely the spirit had used Garen to fulfill its will, without Garen knowing this.

His horror mixed with a moment of rage. It was one thing for She-Who-Foresees to enlist him for some task. He wanted this from Her, accepted happily this part of their relationship which had so vexed Yura. But another spirit doing the same thing felt like a violation, or worse—a rape of his will.

He sat with this feeling, seething, until he noticed something else, an odd sense of peace that surprised him. And then he thought more on it, calming. It couldn't have been Ul'dre'na who possessed him. He had no relationship with the spirit and was anyway too strong to be jumped by a spirit. And he would have foreseen this, would have known to protect himself ahead of time if another spirit was trying to manipulate him.

So all this meant it was actually *Her*. She-Who-Foresees had woken him, guided his hands to mix the poisons and his feet to cross the courtyard in the middle of the night. He'd poisoned the horses because She'd seen they needed to be poisoned.

There was never any malice in Her actions, only always necessity. The horses were innocent, but as Garen increasingly understood, the men who rode them absolutely were not. They needed to not have horses, and Ronúr needed to believe the old elder had caused their death. Garen had caused both to happen.

He still didn't understand why, though. They were two days out from the city by horse, which meant at least six days by foot. And they were going further up into the mountains, further into the forests. And with this thought more flooded his mind: without the horses, they wouldn't be able to carry all the supplies they'd taken with them. And even if they took what they could and left the surplus at the villa, there wasn't enough for a return journey by foot.

"We're not all coming back," Garen said, speaking aloud the unavoidable truth crashing into his mind. He would have foreseen they would need more supplies if six men would be returning from the journey. Even if they found their prey tonight, there wasn't enough. Maybe for three, not for six.

Garen thought immediately of Uric. Ronúr had beaten Thalyn because he'd sent Uric away. Maybe Ronúr had thought Uric would die while scouting, was furious that Thalyn had sent him to that death. But Ronúr had shown no anger about the lost horses, and this had worried Uric. So Ronúr must know —or was maybe even intending—that they'd not all return either.

Garen tried to calm his shaking hands enough to thread the needle he'd need to sew together the skin on Thalyn's scalp. He missed several times; then, breathing deeply, finally got the thick filament through. He cut off a length, knotted the two ends together, then put the needle down and began mixing the herbs to clean Thalyn's wounds.

The water had boiled. He put aside a portion to mix a poultice of bone-mend, another portion to make a paste for the wounds, and with the rest of the water he soaked a cloth to clean away the clotted blood from Thalyn's face and scalp.

Working this way helped calm him. He could do nothing about what was coming, or nothing that he'd not already done without knowing. "You already always have what ye'r gonna need," Yura had taught him. This was what it meant to be a

Provisioner, being prepared for whatever would happen even without any idea of what would actually arrive. Though rarely was the future something which worried him, Garen did rather wish he at least this time knew what was coming.

The work on Thalyn passed quickly. The worst wound was the one on his scalp, but it wasn't deep and there was enough skin remaining for him to sew it shut easily. There was no damage to Thalyn's eye itself, so he didn't need to drain the swollen flesh around it. He spread the poultice of bone-mend last, then tied a length of cloth from Thalyn's own shirt around his chest to keep it in place.

No one appeared while he worked, though he heard Jord and Huwvyn talking to each other elsewhere in the house, too low and distant for Garen to catch their meaning. Ronúr hadn't returned, likely not wanting to confront the mess he'd made of Thalyn's face until Garen had finished.

Ronúr's violence against his lover—it was clear they were lovers—was terrible. But less comprehensible and even more terrible was Ronúr's suppressed sense of guilt over the violence. He'd beaten Thalyn for lying to Uric and sending him off alone, undermining his authority, whatever that meant. It seemed to Garen that there was probably something else between them, but he couldn't guess what. Possibly something to do with Uric himself.

Garen stood up, looking over his work. As Ronúr had said—though also probably had asked—Thalyn would survive. At least from these wounds, anyway.

CHAPTER TEN

They didn't set off to the abbey until well past midday, because Ronúr hadn't returned. He didn't say where he'd gone, and no one (including Thalyn, now conscious and in a wretched humor) asked him.

Thalyn had come to earlier, spitting a lot of blood from his mouth and cursing his lost teeth. Jord and Huwvyn stayed clear of him, but Garen lingered close to make sure the stitches did not tear out.

Garen had braced for Thalyn's anger, but was surprised to find Thalyn didn't intend to rage at him for telling Ronúr what he'd done. Instead, Thalyn listened to Garen's directions to keep the bone-mend poultice wet and to not touch his eye or the wound on his scalp.

"You'll have to wash the wound tomorrow, and don't sleep on your back tonight. And sorry about your teeth. No one can fix that."

Thalyn nodded silently, then asked, "where's Ronúr?"

Garen shrugged. "He left but he didn't take his pack. So I assume he'll be back."

Something passed across Thalyn's face that Garen thought looked like pain, but not the pain from his wounds. "He went after Uric?"

Again, Garen shrugged. "He didn't say. He seemed..." and here Garen stopped himself, because he was about to lie. And he didn't know why he was about to lie, but now he couldn't think of a truth to replace it with.

"Seemed what?" Thalyn demanded aggressively.

"He seemed sorry he hurt you."

With those words, Thalyn's face softened. He merely nodded in reply, but Garen was certain the lie's affect was much greater than he'd expected.

Perhaps it wasn't really a lie, or a full one. The truth would have been longer and more complicated, certainly—Ronúr had seemed shocked and angry that he'd hurt Thalyn, which in other people, those with at least some sense of themselves, would have manifested as regret.

When Ronúr did finally return—without Uric—he didn't speak to Thalyn or any of them except to say, "we leave now." They had already been ready, having sorted through what could be carried from the horse's packs while they'd waited for Ronúr's return.

The five left the villa in silence, and they kept that silence for most of the afternoon. The path to the abbey was harder than the road behind them had been, ascending sharply in some places through overgrown forest and over rockfalls from the high cliffs to their left. The trail wouldn't have been much easier for the horses, and in several places they would have had to dismount regardless, but Garen's cramping and tired shoulders made him rue more than once that he'd killed them.

The short bits of conversation which did break the silence gave Garen no more sense of what Ronúr actually intended to do, nor why Thalyn had sent Uric ahead against Ronúr's wishes, nor why that had made Ronúr angry. Huwyn remained completely silent on the road except once to tell Jord to "fuck off with the noise."

Garen had wanted to say the same thing to the man. He grunted, muttered a lot, gestured with his hands occasionally against the air like he was swatting away insects no one else saw. "Stop looking at me," he'd abruptly said once, and then everyone looked at him. But they'd not been looking at him before that, and Jord didn't notice their attention now on him. He'd been talking to a memory, or a spectre, or to himself.

From that moment on, Garen watched Jord whenever he could do so without drawing the man's attention. He would be silent, acting as normally as all the others, then suddenly jolt, look around him, mutter, and then just as quickly relax as if nothing had interrupted his thoughts.

Huwvyn had told Garen that Jord talked about killing children in his sleep. "What you bury wakes when you sleep, or in your body," Yura had once told him. Perhaps that was Jord's problem—he'd buried some memory, or some guilt. It was still there, waking as he slept, waking in his body.

Garen shuddered at the thought. Jord had killed children then. And Uric had killed priests, and Huwvyn's brother and who knew how many others. And Ronúr—Ronúr had beaten Thalyn to near death: perhaps this was nothing to him compared to what else he had done.

Looking away from Jord and the others and towards the ancient trees flanking their path, Garen shook his head and sighed. He was provisioning murderers, and had himself murdered horses the night before. Every one of Yura's warnings about She-Who-Foresees flooded back to him, filling him with revulsion.

What had She gotten him into? And why had he not thought to question Her?

His thoughts fell back into silence and a morbid calm as they stopped to eat by a ruined bridgehouse. Part of its roof had collapsed, its door lay broken and shattered on the threshold, and ferns and birch saplings grew in the uneven stones of its walls.

The bridge beyond it was fortunately in better shape, a short stone-work arched bridge spanning a deep, forested ravine through which a clear glacial river flowed, swollen still from late-summer melts. Only a few blocks on each side were missing from the low wall flanking its narrow path, and the paving stones were fitted tight enough that only a few small tufts of grass had managed to find purchase between them.

In another time, one when he had not found himself in the unwitting company of brutal killers, Garen imagined he might find such a place beautiful. He tried to anyway, breathing in the cold mist that sometimes swept up to them from the river below, letting his eyes wander from the ancient masonry to the dark green of the forests below and beyond.

"Who built this?" Garen asked, after cutting off enough pieces of dried meat and hard bread for the other men. "Is this before Verych, too?"

He had expected Huwvyn to answer, but instead it was Ronúr. "Dead people. Enemies of the king."

Jord grunted, Thalyn said nothing. Huwvyn answered. "Monks from the abbey ahead. They died from the plague."

"Old stones mean nothing," Ronúr spat. "Nothing will outlast Verych."

Garen shuddered, then hoped no one had noticed. *'Nothing will outlast Verych'* was what the soldiers said, and the priests of the city, and his landlord, and all those engorged on warlust he'd tried so hard to avoid on the streets, in the markets, or at the taverns.

He said nothing more, nor did the others. They ate in silence, refilled their flasks from a small stream cascading down the cliffs above them into the ravine below, then crossed over the bridge and further up the sloping paved path up the mountain.

Hours later, the abbey's stone towers and high walls appeared suddenly through the trees on their ascent, pale stones looming almost gold in the fading autumn light. It looked to Garen less like a place of learning or an ascetic commune and more a fortress, though the closer they came in view of its ornate masonry work, Garen began to decide it was likely both.

The trees alongside the path also changed, trunks and branches weaving with each other. They looked shaped, trained into growing intertwined to create a living wall. As along the bridge, the paving stones were fitted too tightly with each other to allow for grasses and other plants to grow between them, and even the trees roots appeared unable to upheave them.

Only Garen betrayed any wonder at the place. Huwvn, Thalyn, and Ronúr were silent. Even Jorn had ceased his erratic gestures and grunts.

"Where's Uric?" Ronúr said, laying down his heavy pack on the ground, but keeping the long shoulder bag with the strange chest strapped to him.

Garen didn't see him either, then noticed that Ronúr had directed the question to Thalyn. Thalyn scowled for a brief moment, then shrugged, laid down his own pack, and strode past them towards the abbey's gates.

Thalyn disappeared from their sight, and the four of them waited. Jorn and Huwvyn sat, but Garen was too worried to follow them and instead stood along with Ronúr.

The time passed uncomfortably. Without distraction, Jorn's mutterings started again, Huwvyn sighed, irritated, and Garen yawned from fatigue. Ronúr, however, remained silent, expectant, poised as if ready to fight.

Garen saw Thalyn first, but didn't see the expression on his face since he was too busy staring at the bloodied, torn shirt in his hand. Garen gasped, but Ronúr's growl drowned it out.

"Where is he?" Ronúr said again, his voice raging.

Thalyn kept walking towards them, defiant in the face of Ronúr's terror. If anything, he looked almost triumphant.

"I'm going to guess by the all the blood inside that he's dead."

Jorn and Huwvyn stood up, eyeing Ronúr's fists and the engorged cables of vein in his neck. Garen felt paralyzed, too shocked to get out of the way of whatever was about to happen between Thalyn and Ronúr.

"You prick," Ronúr barked, reaching for his sword.

"You'd rather it had been me?" Thalyn said back, his voice surprisingly even. "Uric was an idiot, but the only better fighter than him here is you."

Despite the whelm of grief Garen felt that Uric was dead and the unsettling horror at finding himself even more alone now, Garen kept his wits about him long enough to notice Thalyn's stroking of Ronúr's ego had worked. The raging man suddenly calmed, let go of the hilt of his sword, and grunted.

"What killed him then?" Huwvyn asked.

Thalyn shrugged. "Don't know. I don't see his body, just this shirt and more blood than a gutted pig."

Garen tried not to retch at the idea, tried to keep calm, tried not to let the others know he wanted to both scream and cry. Instead he turned away, facing back towards the path from which they'd come, and whispered a quick prayer.

"Let's go see it then," Ronúr ordered.

The others followed him, but Garen called back, "I'll stay here if that's alright."

Ronúr strode heavily to Garen, grabbed his shirt in his fist, and pulled him slightly off the ground. "I'm not losing a Provisioner along with a soldier. Do what I say."

Garen nodded, his chest heaving. "Okay," he sputtered, then picked up his packs and followed after them into the gate of the abbey. Despite his earlier composure, this time he actually retched when he saw the blood, a dark pool of it just within the entrance illuminated by fading light filtering through a high window.

The blood had clotted, looked less like liquid and more like a thin, syrupy sheen across the stone. To the right of them the blood smeared, like something—or someone—had been dragged through it into another room.

"His shirt was here," Thalyn pointed, and Garen felt even more sickened by the man's gloating tone.

Ronúr barked questions. "His body? His pack?"

Thalyn pointed to the side room. "What's left of his ruck is in there, but it's been torn open. Too dark to find his body though."

Huwvyn struck a lantern, and he, Ronúr, and Thalyn walked to the other room. Garen stayed with Jord, who was quietly talking to himself. He listened both to the mad man and the other men's voices, trying to make sense of what they were all saying rather than trying to make sense of how he was feeling.

They came back, dragging Uric's blood-soaked pack, but not his body. "We'll look when there's morning light," Ronúr said. "Huwvyn, take the boy to get wood for a fire. We'll sleep here tonight. Jord, you're first watch."

Huwvyn and Jord both nodded, but Garen, numb, tried to bite back the maddening mix of grief and terror and said nothing.

"Let's go," Huwvyn said, grabbing Garen's shoulder. It was far from a gentle gesture, but regardless it felt to Garen more human than anything else that had yet happened.

Garen followed the man into the gateyard and down the wide stone steps of the abbey's entrance. The trees were too close on either side of them to enter into the forest, but following a narrow path along the abbey's wall they found a woven gap of branches forming an arch and, past it, a small path leading further into the wood.

They soon found several large fallen branches, old enough to be dry but not so old to be useless for the fire. In the shock of Uric's death, Garen had forgotten to take his hatchet. Huwvyn gave him the one he wore on his belt and stood watch while Garen cut the wood into smaller logs.

The sound of the axe against the wood felt profane in the silence, or maybe it was the silence itself that was profane, and Garen interrupted both with a question. "What do you think killed Uric? The wolf?"

Huwvyn grunted. "No. The same men who killed my brother. Men from Arras."

Garen gulped back the response he almost gave. *Uric had killed Veln,* or at least claimed to have. But telling Huwvyn this would lead to awful questions Garen didn't want to answer, especially how he came to that knowledge in the first place.

Garen continued chopping, tried to gather his wild thoughts into something coherent. "So we're being followed?"

Huwvyn nodded. "The king sent half of his personal guard away into the mountains. Of course Arras would try to kill us."

The axe fell from his hand at those words. He fumbled to pick it up, his hands shaking. "You're the kings's bodyguards?"

Huwvyn shrugged. "Feeling important, boy?"

Garen sighed. "Feeling like I'm in danger, I guess. Two of you are already dead."

The man grabbed the axe from Garen's hands. Garen flinched, expecting to be hit, but instead Huwvyn began chopping the branches. "You're too slow, boy. Keep watch."

Garen stepped back and scanned the trees around them. The place was quiet, beautiful even, and the path they'd taken ascended further towards a small stone structure that looked to be some sort of shrine.

"What's the history of this place?" Garen asked. He preferred to keep Huwvyn talking rather than face the dark, silent questions in his head.

"Beast fuckers," Huwvyn laughed. "Monks who worshiped animals so much they had sex with them."

"They went through a lot of work building this abbey in the middle of nowhere just to fuck animals," Garen replied, looking again towards the shrine.

"Yeah—well..." Huwvyn stopped, appearing to think. "They're all dead anyway. That happens when you oppose Verych."

"Huh," Garen said, lacking anything better to say. "So they were killed?"

Huwvyn heaved several large logs over to Garen. "You ask a lot of questions."

He shrugged, feeling suddenly bold. "How long was Uric part of the guard?"

Huwvyn suddenly threw the axe past Garen into a nearby tree. "Two years. Best man we had."

Garen walked to the tree and tried to dislodge the axe, but the man had thrown it really hard. He struggled a bit, then finally pulled it out and handed it back to Huwvyn. "You lost both your brother and your friend. I'm sorry."

Huwvyn suddenly pushed Garen backwards against the tree, then pinned him there with his forearm and his full body weight against Garen's chest. "Veln was a prick and Uric wasn't my friend. You need to stop talking. Only thing stopping me from gutting you right now is that Ronúr won't want to fuck your corpse."

Though he could barely breathe, Garen's fear turned to hysteria and he began laughing. "Ronúr wants to fuck me? That's what you needed a Provisioner for?"

Huwvyn spat in his face. "The rest of us would have split you open already if it weren't for Ronúr demanding first go."

Garen was still laughing, then turned his eyes again towards the shrine. "You're all no different than these monks were, huh? Rutting each other like boars."

Huwvyn spat in his face again, and Garen jolted. Huwvyn's other hand had grabbed Garen's crotch with a vise grip.

"What's this hard cock then, boy?"

For a moment Garen tried to fight the arousal, then didn't see the point. "Yeah, I'd not say no."

Huwvyn laughed, then licked the side of Garen's cheek. The feel of the man's beard against his face and the heavy scent of Huwvyn's breath sent heat through his entire body, but Garen pulled away.

"Would rather have you first, but I guess you'll have to clean me off and use me after Ronúr's done."

"Fuck," Huwvyn grunted, then suddenly regained his senses. "Let's get this wood back."

"Okay," Garen said, trying to calm himself down too. He gathered up as many logs as he could carry, then followed after Huwvyn, turning one more time to glance back at the shrine and shudder at the sense of something watching him.

CHAPTER ELEVEN

No one seemed to notice or care how long it had taken Huwvyn and Garen to gather the wood, because Ronúr and Tha-lyn were arguing. Jord stood outside the gate, smoking, pretending not to listen. He also pretended not to see the two men arrive.

"What're they on about?" Huwvyn asked, his voice low.

Jord shrugged. "You think I'm an idiot? I'm not going near them."

Garen couldn't make out their words from where he stood, and Huwvyn didn't press further, so he contented himself with building the fire, staying out of everyone's way, and thinking about all the questions now filling his head.

Though Huwvn's scent still lingered in his beard, his earlier arousal had chilled, no longer distracting him from the deep dread of Uric's death. That sudden desire had felt like an odd betrayal, anyway—these men were brutal murderers, and more so the king's personal guard. Garen thought somewhere he should be disgusted by the idea of sex with any of them, especially Ronúr.

But he wasn't. Actually, the moment Huwvyn mentioned Ronúr intended to "use" their Provisioner before the rest of them had a turn on him, Garen had fought off an upwell of excitement.

Yura may have prepared him very well for everything else, but for this she'd said nothing. Garen wished more than anything to talk to her right now, tell her everything that was happening, demand advice he nevertheless knew she wouldn't be able to give.

He could ask Her tonight. But what might She tell him? Nothing more than She already had, which was only images of what he would need, visions of what had passed before, why the eldress had died and how the villages in these mountains had become emptied. Nothing about why he suddenly desired these men as much as he loathed them, nor what had happened to Uric, nor to the monks in this abbey.

"The shrine," Garen whispered aloud, involuntarily.

"What, boy?" Jord spat on the ground, just missing Garen.

"Nothing," he muttered back, and returned to his thoughts. He'd felt something, or some presence, watching him while he and Huwvyn gathered wood. Huwvyn for his part hadn't even glanced in its direction, so he'd probably not felt it.

Garen would need to go to the shrine somehow. How, though? He doubted the Arras assassins would care that he wasn't actually part of the kings's guards if they caught him. And they must still be nearby. They'd kill him even easier than they'd killed Uric.

The kindling sparked under the logs just at the moment he understood another problem. Huwvyn had said men from Arras had killed Veln, but Uric had claimed he himself had. One of them was wrong. Either Uric had been merely boasting, or Huwvyn didn't realise or suspect Uric had killed his brother.

If Uric had, then he had betrayed the other members of the guard. And Uric had enlisted Garen in finding out what Ronúr was really planning, meaning that Uric was a traitor, maybe even from Arras himself. That would be a long game, Garen mused, a spy getting into the king's personal guard, fighting along side them for years, gaining their trust and then only now betraying them.

Maybe it was less complicated than that. Maybe Uric had been who he said he was but then turned, was bought off by Verych's enemies. He was a traitor or a liar, or maybe both. Either way, Garen wished he'd not gone off and died on him before he got to discover the truth.

He stepped back from the fire, now burning strongly. "Any of you seen a spring or a well? I haven't seen one yet. Maybe up by that shrine?"

Jord gestured with his hand. "There's a pumpwell in the gate-yard. Water's good, too."

Garen tried not to look disappointed. He'd have to find another excuse to go up to the shrine, then.

After the horses had died, the others had at least divided up the camp supplies in their own packs rather than making Garen carry it all. But while easier to travel that way, Garen would first need to collect the scattered food, pots, and plates from each bag before cooking.

The pot, he regretted, had been in Ronúr's pack. Though their arguing had quieted to angry grunts, Garen was not in any sort of mood to interrupt them. Still, there was nothing else to do if anyone wanted to eat this evening, so he crossed the gateyard, entered through the main doors of the abbey, skirted the pool of Uric's blood, and timidly made his way towards the hall where he'd heard them arguing.

Garen froze at the doorway, staring dumbly. Thalyn and Ronúr had stopped their arguing completely and decided to settle the dispute more amicably.

The first thing which transfixed Garen was Thalyn's face pressed flat against the stone wall, his head turned away from the doorway as Ronúr bit his ear. Garen could see the man's thighs, but only barely, as Ronúr's massive, muscled legs kept thrusting them—along with the rest of Thalyn's body—into the wall.

Neither of them had taken off their shirts, but Garen had already seen Ronúr shirtless, his scars and tattoos dripping with water from the fountain at the ruined villa. What Garen could now see was even better. Their leader, the captain of the king's bodyguard, had an ass of pure muscle and hair, like the hind of a horse.

Garen's breath caught in his throat. He couldn't retreat and didn't dare interrupt them. Ronúr kept thrusting, slamming Thalyn's body against the stones, all the while growling to match Thalyn's guttural groaning.

Despite all the wisdom screaming at him not to, Garen stepped sideways, shifting his perspective for a better view of Ronúr's ass. What he saw instead entranced him even more:

Ronúr's scrotum, swinging with each thrust, slapping against Thalyn's as if it were also fucking him.

Garen bit his lip, tried to think of something else, tried to move away. All his terror of Ronúr became lust, an absurd but thrilling desire to be in Thalyn's place, to feel what he felt, to feel broken open by such virile rage.

His own cock responded, and he could feel a slick dripping down the side of his leg. He shouldn't be here, shouldn't be watching, yet he could not move. Desire and lust paralyzed him in place.

Ronúr's grunting was louder, his thrustings faster. Thalyn groaned, begging the man for more of it. Garen could see Thalyn's arm jerking, but couldn't see what his hand was holding or the engorged flesh that was turning him inside out. Garen wanted to move, wanted to get a better view, but there was no way he could do so without being more in their sight.

Too late, Garen noticed that Ronúr had stopped biting Thalyn's ear, was using his arm now to pin the man's neck in place, and had turned his face to watch the man who watched them. Garen wanted to run away when he saw Ronúr's eyes on him, but he was not even more rooted in place.

Ronúr said nothing, only stared at Garen without stopping his work on Thalyn. Ronúr's face didn't change for what felt like an eternity, and then suddenly his mouth twitched into a feral, tooth-filled smile that felt more animal then human. He let out a series of growling shouts, tensing his ass, his legs, and his back, and then pushed himself entirely against Thalyn twice before throwing him down to the ground.

"Still not as good as Uric," Ronúr spat to Thalyn, then turned his body so that Garen could see his still pulsing cock. "But I think our Provisioner is ready for his turn."

"Fuck you!" Thalyn shouted, turning on his back to face Ronúr. Garen gaped at the prone form of Thalyn, naked from the waist down, his body and cock still heaving with lust.

But the mention of Uric pulled Garen out of his intoxication. He shook his head. He was sure he looked like a fool, but he didn't care. "I came to get the pot. We need water." And then, surprised at himself, he added, "but that was nice to watch, thanks."

Thalyn didn't stand from the floor when he spoke. "Ronúr will need another hour before he can go again. I guess he'll have to let me have first go."

Ronúr growled at Thalyn, but Thalyn didn't flinch. "Let's ask the boy who he wants first."

Garen was tiring of this. "Second, you mean? Uric already had me in the village."

Thalyn laughed suddenly, then kicked Ronúr in the leg. "Told you we couldn't trust Uric anymore."

Ronúr pulled his trousers up past his boots, far enough up his legs to stride over to Garen, glaring. "You're lying."

Ronúr towered a full half of a head over Garen, but something in his post-orgasm weakness gave Garen the courage to continue. "Want me to describe it for you? I didn't know you were saving me for yourself otherwise I would have told him no. But anyway, I need the pot."

Thalyn answered for Ronúr, his voice triumphant, almost giddy. "His pack is over there." Then, to Ronúr again, Thalyn said, "I was right."

Ronúr barked back at Thalyn, "I'll knock the rest of your teeth out if you don't shut up." He then hoisted his trousers fully up, belted them, then stormed off out of the room.

"Well, then," Thalyn said, stroking himself. "Want to finish me off? Though I guess I owe you my throat at least for all you've done for me."

Garen grinned. "Thanks, but really. It's getting dark. And besides, I'm the reason Ronúr knew you sent Uric off. Where's the pot?"

Thalyn stood, pulled up his trousers, and belted them without putting his cock back in. "Ronúr's pack, there. Uric really fucked you, huh?"

Garen had to cross the room to get to Ronúr's rucksack. He paused briefly as he came close to Thalyn, then passed by him and walked to the corner. He felt Thalyn watch him as he passed, heard his heavy breathing

"Yeah. Not too well though. I guess he's better underneath you, huh? You had him?"

Thalyn spat. "Wouldn't let that traitor anywhere near me. I think he killed Veln."

Garen shrugged, unbuckling the leather bindings on the pack. He was trying not to look like he was looking at something else—Ronúr had left his shoulder bag, and with it the long chest, next to his pack.

Garen didn't think he could get closer to it without Thalyn noticing, and he didn't think Thalyn would answer his questions about it without something in return. Garen turned, facing him, and smiled. "I'm already on my knees I guess. Need help?"

Thalyn grinned, stood, strode up to Garen, then slapped his pole against Garen's face. "I'd love to choke you. But I don't have many more teeth to spare."

Garen laughed. "Okay. But tell Ronúr to hurry up with me so I can get my turn with you."

Thalyn wagged his cock twice before hitting Garen on the cheek with it. "Thought so. I saw you looking at me since you arrived."

Garen nodded. "At least let me taste."

"I got something better for you," Thalyn grunted. His hand disappeared down the back of his trousers, then reappeared, covered in Ronúr's cum. "Open your mouth."

Garen didn't have time to comply before Thalyn's hand had already pried his lips open, forcing his fingers coated in Ronúr's man seed onto his tongue.

Garen licked it away, slightly biting Thalyn's fingers just enough to make the man know what he wanted. "Rather it were yours," he said.

Thalyns cock throbbed. "You little dog. You'll get it. But I'm gonna go clean up now. Hurry up and make us our dinner."

Garen fumbled more with the pack as he listened to Thalyn leave. He turned his head to check, saw he was really gone, then squatted over Ronúr's shoulder bag.

The chest inside was heavy, and the moment he moved it he heard what sounded like the rattling of chains. Worried the noise would draw the others attention, he placed it back down. HE then tried to slip the bag off of the chest as far as he could.

It was too dark to see it well, but he felt a lock immediately, then ran his hands along the wood and traced an engraving. A rune of some sort, a black one, a rune of binding and trapping.

Garen removed his hand quickly, whispering a prayer of banishing to push away the sudden sick feeling in his mind, then slipped the bag over the chest, grabbed the pot, and headed back out to the gateyard.

CHAPTER TWELVE

Even after the banishing prayer, the shape of the rune haunted Garen. Before filling the pot from the pumpwell he ran the cold water over his hands, then brought some to his mouth to rinse out Ronúr's taste. Then he washed his hands again, and then again, and yet still the dread feeling would not subside.

If the others saw his ritual there they said nothing, and Garen was glad of the silence. If anything they seemed to ignore him.

The dread stayed with him as he hung the pot of water over the fire and filled it with dried deer meat and the onions and turnips he'd traded for in the first village. The dread stayed with him as he watched the water boil, as he added the barley he'd brought and the late nettles he'd picked along the walk. And it was still there as he rummaged through his own pack, secretively opening the chest Yura had provisioned him with and added what he would call "cooking herbs" if any of them has asked.

They didn't ask, though, or say anything at all to him except to ask when the food would be ready.

"Not long," he replied, surprised at the chill in his voice.

It was the rune, probably. He shouldn't have touched it, or shouldn't have left after touching it without finding out which one it was so he could properly counter it.

It was the rune, but it was also something else, or everything else. What he had said to Huwvyn, to Ronúr, what he had tried to do with Thalyn. "This *isn't* me," he whispered to himself low enough that the sound of the fire drowned out his words.

It wasn't him, at least when he was aware of what he was doing. Waking up in the barn next to the man he thought was Sorn, now Uric—he'd thrown his shirt into the water that night, jumped into the river to get it. That wasn't Garen, or the usual Garen. And he'd obviously seduced the man, else he'd not have woken next to him the next morning, drink-sick yet still aroused.

The other times? He'd told Yura it had been three, but now giving serious account there had been at least ten. He'd woken in inns, once on the deck of a docked ship, several times in the houses of others, once in the bed of a man being screamed at by a wife who returned a day too early from a visit to her sister. There was the morning with the two soldiers in a dock house, and a morning trudging back home through snow from the noble's quarter, and a morning spent untying a merchant from bedposts before walking home through a soft spring rain.

He didn't regret any of the men he woke to. Nor did any of the men—even the married one—seem to regret him. At least twice he was offered pay, once was begged for another meet-

98

ing (the soldiers), and never once shunned or pushed out. It was always he who left, perplexed at the mystery of how he'd come to wake there, embarrassed they remembered his name and he did not.

He stirred the stew, made a show of tasting it and frowning in case they were watching, then added the herbs he'd selected. Rank setwall, violet mohn pods, mayweed flowers, motherwort, and dried sweet hops. It'd not be enough to knock the men to sleep immediately, but exactly enough they'd fall into it gradually without suspecting there was anything odd about being so tired.

It felt a bit foolish to be poisoning them tonight, with whomever—or whatever—killed Uric likely nearby. They'd not wake on their own under their influence, nor to a loud noise like the sound of him screaming for help, though he could still wake them with a hard push. Garen had to risk it, though. He needed to get to the shrine, though he didn't understand why yet.

They ate quickly without speaking. Garen had ladled enough of the stew into his bowl before adding the herbs that no one questioned him when he took only a little more of it, nor were they even giving him any attention at all. Maybe it was Uric's death, or Garen's revelation about what he and Uric had done (only half a lie, chronologically false yet still true), or the strange quiet of the abbey. Whatever it was, the men all seemed sullen, lost in their thoughts.

Ronúr finally broke the silence. "I'll take first watch, Jord. You're second, then Huwvyn, then Thalyn."

Garen heard an odd tenderness in Ronúr's voice when he said Thalyn's name. He was favoring the man; last watch meant he would get uninterrupted sleep.

Garen began collecting their bowls to wash. Ronúr grabbed his shoulder as he took his. "You're on first with me. I've got some questions for our Provisioner."

Garen glanced at Thalyn, who returned his glance without expression. None of the men said anything else, but Garen could feel they all knew what Ronúr intended to do.

Carrying the bowls and pot to the pumpwell through the now dark gateyard, Garen returned to his earlier questions. None of this was him, maybe, *but it was also him*. He wasn't a poisoner of horses or of men, but he had now done both. He was no virile rake, but here he was wolfishly playing off these men's lust for him.

He was none of those things but he was also all of those things. To his friends he was a slightly-boring, quiet, and passive man who kept too much to himself, to his books, to his shrines and prayers. To Yura he was a bit more, a stubborn youth who'd been her student and like a son, but not very world-wise and anyway he'd never even experienced love.

To himself, Garen was all those things others thought about him, and not much more. He wasn't the man who walked home after nights with attractive men whose names he'd never bothered to learn. Regardless, though, Garen had done those things: this was also him.

The only thing he and all those others would agree on is that he was a Provisioner. This he knew deeply, felt fully. There'd never been a question in his head from the moment Yura had convinced him, and meeting She-Who-Foresees had only increased this certainty. He could see before others, could—no, would always—know what was needed. He would never find himself in a situation he wasn't already prepared for.

"Oh," he said aloud, rinsing the last of the bowls. "*I guess I know what I'm doing.*" And then he laughed, relief and a peaceful joy welling up inside him.

"*I know what I'm doing,*" he said again, and laughed more. He wanted to shout it, to howl those words into every room of the empty abbey, howl them into the forests around them, howl them into the mountains.

He knew what he was doing, though he didn't know what that was yet. He just did, and what he did was precisely what he needed to do and needed to have done.

He looked around, still laughing. No one was watching him, so he laughed a little longer, finished rinsing the pot, and then returned to the fire by the gate. The others were still sitting there. They turned to look at him awkwardly when he arrived. They'd been talking about him probably, but Garen didn't care.

"Alright I'm off," Huwvyn said, standing up. Jord and Thalyn followed his gesture silently. The three passed by Garen without making any sign of what they'd been discussing. Ronúr was still sitting by the fire, staring into the flames as if searching for something there, and so Garen sat next to him and stared, too.

They passed several minutes this way in silence before Garen decided to speak. "You wanted to ask me some questions?"

Ronúr didn't reply. Garen turned to look at his face, flickering firelight illuminating his beard and reflecting in his eyes. The light softened him a bit, made him look more human, less murderous.

Garen turned back towards the flames. Ronúr was much bigger than the others, taller, broader, built more like an ox or a bear. There was more to the man than the other men: the herbs would take a little longer to work in his body.

"If you don't want to ask me questions, then I'll ask you one." Despite his epiphany at the pumpwell, the boldness in Garen's voice when he said this surprised him.

"What, then?" Ronúr said, sounding not irritated but merely bored.

"Who killed Uric? What are we watching for?"

Ronúr grunted. "Don't know. Our enemies shouldn't know we're here unless someone betrayed us, and anyway shouldn't have gotten here so quickly before us. Maybe the hex from that bitch in the village brought them faster."

Garen could hear that Ronúr was telling the truth: he really didn't know. Maybe that's what the men were talking about before he arrived at the fire, not about their Provisioner but about the unknown enemy stalking them.

It wouldn't have been the hex from the elder, though, unless already men had been waiting in the abbey for the emperor's guard to arrive. It had been too dark to search further, they hadn't even found Uric's body yet, let alone signs left by whomever killed him. But if they had been waiting here before them they would have left obvious signs. Even the pumpwell had needed to be primed when they arrived: no one had used it for days at least.

Garen mused further: *that meant Uric hadn't used it, either.* He'd had no time, was killed so soon after he arrived he'd not been able to refill his water skins. It had been quick, he'd been jumped, killed, and his body dragged off, his pack torn open and belongings scattered, no more than four hours before his companions had arrived.

Ronúr had been silent for a minute, then growled, "you got more questions, boy?"

Garen turned to face the man again. "A serious one, yeah. Do I have to get fucked by the all the others here after you? You're the only one who looks worth taking."

Ronúr laughed, not unpleasantly. He reached out his hand, ran his fingers through Garen's hair, then grabbed a clump of it and pulled. "You're right. And no. If I say you're mine, they won't touch you."

Garen nodded. "Besides Uric."

Ronúr suddenly tugged Garen's hair, jerking his head backward, exposing his throat to the man's face. Garen stared back, not bothering to hide the fear welling within him or his sudden short, heavy breathing. Anyway he suspected Ronúr wanted Garen to be afraid, needed him to be, and Garen was happy to comply.

Ronúr opened his mouth and let fall a long stream of spit onto Garen's face. "I would have killed him myself. You're mine, boy."

Ronúr hadn't let go of Garen's hair, so Garen struggled to nod. "Yes. Sire me," he said, guessing what it was that Ronúr really wanted deepest. Watching the way the man had so brutally fucked Thalyn, the aggression with which he treated the other men, then comparing all that to the way he'd looked almost boyishly scared about destroying Thalyn's face and hearing the confusion and fear in his words about Uric's betrayal and his death, Garen had suspected Ronúr doubted his own right-to-dominate.

"*Sire*" had done the trick. Ronúr's body came alive, trilling both with desire and a perverse kind of care. Garen, completely vulnerable, his throat exposed, his head pinned in the man's massive grip, had told him he was worthy to dominate, worthy to be a ruler of other men, worthy of being a grown man's sire.

Ronúr's other hand gripped Garen's throat. He was choking Garen, cutting off the life streams to his head. Garen rolled his eyes upward, moaning. He wasn't scared, but he pretended to be: he'd done this to himself many times, as often for rituals to contact spirits of the dead as to heighten his own solitary orgasms.

"You're mine, boy. Only mine. I'm your sire." Ronúr growled the words, staring into Garen's darkening eyes.

"You're—my sire," Garen moaned back. But he was already elsewhere, his soul traveling past his convulsing body, struggling for air. He was in the forests beyond, looking for the shrine. He was too fast though, flying farther than he had meant to on the winds upon which spirits fly, into the starry night, the lights wheeling about him. And then a cavern, and a man weeping over a woman wrapped in furs, holding in his hands something bloody, a hand bare and slender cut off at the wrist. The man wept, and wept, and wept, then kissed the hand, wrapped it in fur, wailing his grief through the cold stones of the cave and farther, into the cold night illuminated by millions of tiny, blinking lights.

Garen's return was sharp, abrupt, a hard slap against his face. He was no longer under Ronúr but above him, pinned to the big man's chest by one muscled arm while the hand of the other slapped him again.

"You're okay," Ronúr said to him, his voice low and fatherly.

Garen nodded. "You are my sire," he whispered, regaining his breath. "Make me yours."

Ronúr needed no more invitation than that. "Take your clothes off. You're going to ride your sire."

Garen obeyed, trying to find again the image of the woman's severed hand. He unstrapped the leather cords around his ankles that held the trousers' cuffs, unbelted himself, and slipped them off over his boots, while Ronúr pulled Garen's shirt over his head.

"You're perfect, boy," Ronúr said, staring at Garen's naked body straddling his bare chest. He ran his fingers along the thin line of fur from the indent below Garen's chest down to sparse forest around his dripping rod. The man's own, a little longer than Garen's but at least twice as wide, was throbbing against Garen's back impatiently.

Garen ground his balls and inner thighs against Ronúr's stomach, teasing the arrogant warrior while trying not to glance too hard at the small key he saw suspended from the thick silver chain around Ronúr's neck.

Ronúr gritted his teeth, began growling each time Garen ground into him. Garen could see that Ronúr wasn't used to waiting, nor was he accustomed to someone offering him what else he wanted. The captain of the kings's bodyguard was a broken little child inside of all that brutal bravado and violence, craving approval, craving loyalty, craving someone to say what Garen said to him again.

"Sire me. Make me yours."

Garen winced, realising he probably should have spit on Ronúr's cock before letting him inside him. The man had already drained himself into Thalyn, barely had any cock-spit.

Garen's pained expression only made Ronúr more forceful, though, so Garen tried to restrain the pain, to turn it into pleasure, to relax as he slid down.

Ronúr's eyes looked wild, and also heavy. The herbs were beginning to work, and Garen realised he could now make them work even faster. Ronúr felt incredible inside him, but that was all beside the point.

"What the?" Ronúr shouted, confused and in ecstasy. "What are you doing?"

Garen smiled, flexing the muscles in his lower torso again. "Good for you, my sire?"

Ronúr was thrashing. "I've never—how are you doing—uh, oh fuck!"

Garen grinned, clenched again, tightening the muscles within his body like a sheath around the man. "This?"

Ronúr groaned, then wailed, and then pounded his fists against the ground. "You—you, uh—oh gods!"

Garen felt the man erupt within him, and then he clenched once more before lifting off the still-throbbing cock that had impaled him. Ronúr's seed dripping out of him, Garen stood up, then smiled.

Ronúr was snoring.

Garen pulled his trousers on and belted himself together before trying to unclasp the chain around Ronúr's neck. Garen's hands still trembled from the feeling of the man inside of him, but he eventually found the mechanism and released it.

Ronúr had made the rest of this easy. He'd taken the chest with him this time, laying it next to him as he sat at the fire for dinner. Garen didn't have to re-enter the abbey to look for it. He pulled the chest slowly out of the shoulder bag, tilting it slightly towards the fire to get a better look at the rune again.

He stared at it for awhile before clucking his tongue. It was an old rune for a graveyard tree, the yew. Boundings, thresholds between the forests and the towns—nothing particularly malevolent that he could remember. Why he'd felt so affected by it wasn't quite clear to him until he unlocked the long chest and slid the cover off.

Inside was some sort of steel bladed device, shaped in the same manner as the rune, with another rune engraved into it. It was hooked like the rune, and those two hooks looked sharp enough to cut through bone. Garen hesitated, then gently lifted it up. Under the device was a long chain, forged of the same kind of steel, and it looked as if the chain was meant to attach to the hook.

Ronúr made a snorting noise; Garen turned quickly towards the man in fear. He was still asleep though, only choking on his breath mid-snore. Even still, Garen didn't want to risk the possibility of him waking to discover what Garen was doing, so he quickly put the bladed hook back in the chest, closed the cover, locked it, and slid the bag back over it. He then lifted Ronúr's head gently to replace the chain that had held the key.

All that was left now was to go to the shrine, but Garen found himself hesitating. If assassins from Arras had really killed Uric, they were certainly close by. Or if someone—or something—else had killed him, Garen had no reason to believe he himself was safe.

Garen was the only one of the group still awake. By poisoning them to sleep and then leaving, he was likely consigning them to death. Still though—he had to get to the shrine. This he felt inside every bone of his body, and that certainty pushed away his hesitation.

He'd not yet had a vision of his death as all other Provisioners do. Yura hadn't thought this strange, warned him not to let himself think he was somehow invulnerable, but also told him he had quite some time left.

He wasn't going to die this night, he decided. He built up the fire a bit, reasoning that at least its height might convince any attackers that it was being tended, then took off past the gate, down the steps, and tried to find the forest path again. Enough moonlight shone that he could use it to find the woven, natural arch into the wood, but once in the forest he was near blind again.

He closed his eyes, held them shut for several breaths, then re-opened them. Moonlight still filtered through the branches, and in places he could now see it illuminate small parts of the path to the shrine. He stepped cautiously, a few steps at first, then a few more. Then he stopped, closed his eyes again to orient himself.

Opened again, he walked farther up, then stopped abruptly. The path was visible and he could now see part of the shrine in its light. But there was a movement there, subtle, quick, then gone again.

He closed his eyes, opened them, then looked again. He could see nothing there, no more movements. Perhaps it had been his imagination creating movement when there was none, his mind populating the darkness in the absence of definite vision.

No. Movement again, something that looked like a head, a shoulder, shifting slightly near the foot of the shrine.

There was nothing else to do then. He walked further up the path, this time not bothering to close his eyes to reset his vision. He was far from silent, snapping branches as he walked, but Garen didn't think it mattered anymore.

He kept his eyes towards the shrine, watching for movement. The figure there had heard him, moved a bit but not far and not fast. Garen couldn't make out anything more of the person, but he was certain he already knew who it was.

"Uric?" he called out when close enough to be sure his voice would reach the shrine.

"Fuck mate, Garen? Help me."

CHAPTER THIRTEEN

"It's still out there."

In the pale light of the moon, Garen stared at the mangled mess that was now Uric's left arm. He could see bone, blood still dripping, skin hanging like torn cloth. He was glad that was all he could see right now.

"What? The wolf?" Garen asked, ripping off a part of his shirt to tie off Uric's arm better than Uric had. "It attacked you in the abbey?"

Uric winced in pain as Garen untied the previous binding. "No. Here, in the woods. Just up the hill from here. It was watching me for awhile but I think it's gone. It wouldn't come near this shrine."

Garen handed Uric a stick. "Bite this so you don't scream."

Uric opened his mouth and Garen placed it in between the man's teeth before tying off the new tourniquet. Uric thrashed under the pain, but he didn't scream.

"Okay. Your arm is fucked, but at least you're alive. So who attacked you in the abbey?"

Uric let drop the stick from his mouth. "You idiot, I said the woods here. That was boar blood."

Garen shrugged. "I'm pretty sure I'm not the idiot here. You're working for Arras. You killed Veln because he figured that out. And now your arm is mangled."

Uric said through pain-clenched teeth, "no, you're not an idiot."

"And that was boar blood? So you killed a boar to fake your death because Thalyn was on to you."

Uric nodded. "When he convinced Ronúr to send me ahead I realized he knew."

Garen laughed. "Actually, Ronúr smashed his face in pretty bad for that. He never sent you off, Thalyn did."

"Really?" Uric asked. "Fuck."

"They know you were a traitor now, anyway. But they still think you're dead, so at least there's that. Tell me what this whole thing is about. Why do both Verych and Arras want this wolf?"

"You know I can't tell you that. But anyway the wolf attacked me and it's close."

Garen sighed, then grabbed Uric's mangled arm and twisted slightly. "You're still going to treat me like an idiot?"

Uric screamed, then crumpled to the ground. "Fuck you. The wolves are the true rulers of the land. They grant sovereignty, right-to-rule."

Garen let go of Uric's arm. "So killing the last one will do what, exactly?"

Uric growled. "Ronúr's not trying to kill it, he's trying to capture it. Arras wants it alive, too. Verych found a way to trap it with whatever the fuck is in Ronúr's chest. I have to bring it to Arras when they trap it, and you're going to help me."

Garen laughed. "You're still pretending you're in some sort of position of dominance here, huh? Your arm is useless, you can't defend yourself, and there are four men in the abbey and a wolf in the woods who all want you dead. Just fucking stop."

Uric didn't reply, so Garen continued. "Was it Verych or Arras who killed all the other wolves?"

Uric lifted his head to look at Garen. "Verych. The wolves granted the first kings sovereignty. But then the wolves withdrew it when one of the kings summoned the plague to stop a rebellion. So the kings started killing the wolves until about a hundred years ago, when they thought they killed the last one."

Garen looked out into the darkness of the forest, trying to see the wolf that had attacked Uric. "But at least one survived."

Uric nodded. "The people here, the monks in this abbey, protected it. So the king had them tortured until they would tell him where it was and how to find it, and one of them finally broke."

Garen stepped away from Uric, to make sure he was out of reach of the man. "When was this?"

Uric shook his head. "I know what you're thinking. No. It was five years ago. I wasn't part of the guard yet. Only Ronúr and Jord were."

"That explains Jord then. So why do they want it alive now?"

Uric stood up and winced. "It turns out there's another way to get sovereignty from the wolf. You mate with it."

Garen snorted "Ah, so the king's going to rape a wolf to gain power over the land? And you were sent to make sure the king of Arras gets to rape it instead? By the gods I hate all of you."

Disgusted, he turned away from Uric and looked at the shrine. Nothing remained of what once adorned the stone alcove where offerings and prayers were once said. He ran his fingers along the stone, hoping to find engravings he could read by touch, but he found nothing.

"Who was this to?" Garen asked.

"Some beast god, they said. I don't bother with gods."

"They bother with us anyway," Garen replied, then thought hard. He was too stressed to put himself into a trance, and all the herbs and incenses he used to do so when he couln't do it himself were back at the abbey.

He turned back to Uric. "I need you to cut off my breath."

Uric grunted. "What?"

"Here," he said. "Lean against this table. I'll lean back into you." He pressed his back into Uric's chest. "Now, put your hand over my mouth and nose and keep me from breathing no matter how hard I try to stop you."

"What? Why?"

"Uric?" Garen said, pulling Uric's good hand to his face. "Shut up and do this. I need to find out which god was here."

Uric complied, pressing his hand hard against Garen's mouth while pinching his nostrils shut. "When do I stop?"

Garen couldn't answer, and Uric seemed immediately to understand the stupidity of his question. Garen leaned back into him even more, feeling the man's body against his, wishing suddenly he could be close to him like this in some other time, when neither of their lives were in danger.

These thoughts disappeared as the panic set in, the burning feeling in his deflated chest as his lungs demanded air. Heat welled up within his groin and his neck while the skin of his face felt like fire. He started struggling. His animal self took control of his body, freeing the dreaming part from its tether to be chained by something larger.

He felt bear claws scraping the flesh from his chest, then boar tusks piercing past muscle, through bone and into organ, while a wolf gnawed at his groin and ravens pecked out his eyes. His panic was now terror, the certainty of inescapable death. Tooth and claw and tusk and beak ripped apart his suffocating body, while a man, crowned and bloodied and laughing, became each of the animals which consumed him, then man again.

He fell from Uric's grasp onto the ground, heaving, pulling in great draughts of air in choking gasps.

"Well?" Uric asked.

When he'd recovered enough to speak, Garen answered him. "I don't know his name. We call him the Magician-King, and know him by another form. This was for a more feral face of his, older I think."

Uric helped Garen off the ground. "That's useless."

Garen shook his head. "No, it's not. That's why the wolf hasn't attacked you while you're in this shrine. Farmers give him offerings, mostly, and bakers. He protects chickens from foxes, fields from crows, and flour from rats."

Uric grunted again. "That's some kingly magic."

114

Garen turned sharply to face him. "Just fuck off already. And I need to get back to the abbey before they notice I'm gone."

"Prefer their company to mine?"

"If you don't want them to know you're alive, we have no other choice. You should stay here. I'll try to keep them away from the shrine in the morning, and I'll see if I can find a way to leave you food and water. If they're coming this way I'll try to warn you but I won't endanger myself to save your ass."

Uric put his good hand on Garen's shoulder. "I guess that's all I can ask. Either way you need to find out what Ronúr's been carrying around with him.

Garen began to answer, then stopped himself. He didn't trust Uric. "Okay. I don't know how to, but I'll try to find a way."

"He keeps the key around his neck."

Garen nodded. "That won't make it easy then. Again, stay here. If you leave the shrine that wolf will probably kill you."

Then, suddenly softening, Garen added, "don't die right now, okay?"

CHAPTER FOURTEEN

Garen walked along the forest path from the shrine to the abbey, keeping his ears open for any other rustle besides his own feet. The wolf was still out there.

He wasn't afraid, though he didn't know quite know why.

If the wolf had wanted to attack him as he stumbled through the dark, he'd have been an easy target. Bravado, maybe, or foolishness, but Garen didn't think the wolf would attack him at all. He felt protected somehow, perhaps by the Magician-King, perhaps by She-Who-Foresees, or maybe just by not having yet seen his death.

The fire outside the abbey had grown dim, but it still burned. Rove, his trousers still open, snored loudly on his back. Garen stared, breathed, considered what to do. He could let them all sleep through the night, act innocent in the morning, let them think their strange slumber had been another effect of the curse from the dead elder.

Of course, Garen reasoned, it was just as likely they'd blame him instead.

He decided on a better option. He retrieved the small chest of herbs, spit on his hand, and then dusted powdered joint-pine and fly-bane cap on his palm. Spitting again, he rolled the paste between both hands until it formed a tiny pellet. He then walked through the dark to where Jord was sleeping, held the man's nose to force him to open his mouth, then placed the mixture on his tongue before Jord could close his mouth again. Garen then returned quickly to the fire, spit on his hand again, then stuck his fingers into Ronúr's snore-opened mouth before wiping the rest of it from his hands on Ronúr's tunic.

That was all the easy part. The more difficult bit would be pretending to be asleep when Jord arrived, shouting at Ronúr to wake up. He pulled his own trousers down a bit, enough to look like he'd passed out as quickly as Ronúr had, then laid down on the ground, his face turned away from the fire and the abbey, so that Jord couldn't see his eyes twitching when he arrived.

The dose he'd given Jord would wake him up much sooner than it would wake up Ronúr, but it was impossible to tell exactly when that would be. So Garen waited, his eyes open, staring into the dark forest, gathering his scattered thoughts back to him.

He hadn't needed to pretend, though—he'd fell asleep, waking to hear Jord shouting at Ronúr to wake up. Then Garen jolted upright, startled and pained by a kick to his back from Jord.

"Wake up boy. Help me wake Ronúr."

Garen blinked, adding some performance to the fatigue he didn't need to affect. "What? What's happening?"

Jord grumbled. "You heard me. The chief slept on his watch. Looks like he wore himself out on you. He's gonna be angry with who ever wakes him. That's you."

Garen stood up and nodded. He was relieved that Jord had gotten the impression Garen had hoped he would, but he wasn't as happy about being a target for Ronúr's rage.

"Okay, hold on." Garen belted his trousers, then knelt over Ronúr and pinched his nose like he done for Jord.

It worked quickly. Ronúr choked briefly as he gulped in air through his mouth, then, startled, opened his eyes just at the moment Garen removed his hand from the man's nose.

"What the?" he shouted, then sat up, rubbing his eyes. "Why didn't you wake me?"

Jord answered for Garen. "You were both asleep when I got here. The fire's almost out. As least stoke it for me."

Ronúr stood, then stared down at his naked crotch and pulled his own trousers up. "Alright then. Your watch. You'll tell no one I slept."

Jord nodded. "No one. What are we doing with the boy?"

Ronúr turned to Garen. "You watch with Jord, but don't let him in you." Then to Jord he said, "the boy's mine."

Startled by Ronúr's sudden softness, Garen could only answer "okay" and watch him walk back into the darkness of the abbey. Garen then told Jord, "I guess he wasn't so angry."

Jord growled. "If you're on my watch but I don't get to fuck you, you're staying the fuck silent."

Garen shrugged, piled more of the gathered wood on the fire, and sat down with his back to the wall. He stared into the forest, thinking about Uric, then about the wolf, then about the absurd reason why the men wanted to catch the wolf.

He couldn't hold these thoughts for long. He dozed again, then woke to hear Jord shouting at someone. Garen turned, stared at the man: no one was there.

Jord was reacting to his ghosts again, cursing them, chastising them, pleading with them. He uttered something half-formed—"you're fault"—it sounded like, then went silent. Then, again, "dead can't cry," followed by more silence.

Garen sighed and thought about trying to sleep again. Then, he realized the foolish thing he'd done. The knot-pine wasn't the problem: it would only keep Jord awake to counteract the effects of what he had put in the soup. The fly-bane cap was to wake him in the first place, the only good choice of the supplies Yura had given him. But Garen had forgotten Jord wasn't in an even mind, and now he would be hallucinating as well.

Garen breathed deeply several times to wake himself up, then stood. "I'm going to get some water. Need anything?"

Jord didn't reply, nor did he make any sign he knew Garen was there. Instead the man was staring intently into the fire, hypnotized, yelling at memories and ghosts.

"*Fuck,*" Garen said under his breath. He walked between Jord and the fire, gauging for a reaction that didn't come. Garen continued past him, walking towards the pumpwell, contemplating how he might counteract the fly-bane cap.

But there was nothing he could do. All the methods he knew involved purging with water and bitter herb tinctures. He didn't have those herbs, nor the time to make them, and he couldn't see a way to make Jord drink that much water.

"Fuck," he said again, a little louder. He rinsed his hands in the water, then drank from it and kept drinking, more from nervousness than thirst.

The most he could do was keep an eye on Jord, or maybe wake Huwvyn. That seemed the better idea, so he returned again to the chest of herbs, mixed together the knot-pine with less fly-bane cap this time. Then, he returned to the fire to check on Jord again before waking Huwvyn.

Jord was gone.

Garen moved to the other side of the fire and closed his eyes to let them adjust to darkness. Then he opened them again, but could see nothing except the silhouettes of trees and the moonlight upon their leaves. He could see no clear movement and had no guess as to which direction Jord had gone.

Garen called out, then called again. No answer, no sound except the crackling of the fire behind him.

"Fuck," he said one more time, then went back into the abbey, found Huwvyn, put the mixture on his tongue and began shaking him.

It took what felt like an eternity, but the man woke.

"Eh? My watch?"

"Jord just ran into the woods."

Huwvyn grunted. "Fucking Jord. When?"

"Not long ago, probably a few minutes. He was talking to his ghosts."

"He'll be back. Take his watch. I want to sleep more."

Garen sighed, then turned to leave. "Okay. You explain this to Ronúr in the morning."

"Yeah I will," Huwvyn yawned.

Garen started walking back to the fire, then froze. A sharp, inhuman wail rose up from outside the abbey, a scream that felt like it could break bone.

"That's Jord," Huwvyn shouted, then stepped into his boots without binding them and ran past Garen out into the gateyard. "Wake Ronúr!"

Garen did, told him what was happening, and they both ran together to the fire where Huwvyn stood, his axe drawn and his face pale. Just as they arrived, they heard the cry again from the forest.

"Fucking hell what are they doing to him?" Ronúr asked, pulling out his sword.

Garen said nothing, nor did Huwvyn. The three of them stood frozen, unwilling to leave the ring of firelight for the dark shadows of the trees.

The cry rose up one last time, then stopped abruptly, as if suddenly choked out of existence. No other sounds followed except the shallow, quick breaths of the men and the low snapping and hiss of the fire behind them.

No one spoke after that. Garen, Huwvyn, and Ronúr sat together silently by the fire, keeping their ears strained for noise from the forest. The moon set, and not long after the sky lightened again, a somber dawn giving individual form and shape to the trees that for much of the night seemed merely a dark, terrifying wall.

With that dawn came words.

Ronúr spoke first. "When the sun's higher we'll search."

Then to Garen he said, "get us breakfast and go wake Thalyn."

Garen nodded, and asked, "what do you think happened?"

Ronúr shook his head. "Those that got Uric got Jord, damn fool."

He had been thinking about Uric all night after Jord's cries stopped. Uric would have heard them from the shrine. Garen hoped he had stayed there, had not try to flee while Jord died. There was no doubt it was the wolf, at least no doubt for Garen. But he couldn't say this to the others, and didn't think it would matter. They'd find out for themselves soon enough.

This complicated everything. Garen needed to bring water to Uric at the very least, but better food and some healing herbs to keep the blackening from his mangled arm from spreading to the rest of his body. He didn't know how to do this now, except to try to leave while the others searched for Jord's body. If the three of them left together, Garen could maybe have just enough time to help Uric before they returned.

Thalyn woke easily, the effects of the poisoned soup having fully subsided. Garen told him what had happened to Jord, and then gathered the last of their bread, dried boar sausage, half of what remained of their hard cheese, the small sack of dried hyra bean he'd brought with him, and the pot. He boiled the hyra bean while the others ate their fill, leaving very little for him. To retaliate he took most of the steeped hyra, then chewed the bit of sausage and crust of bread they'd left him.

"You stay here, boy," Ronúr barked when they had finished eating. "Keep the fire going. Shout if you see anyone, then run towards us."

Garen nodded, raised the fire a bit, then waited for them to be fully out of sight before grabbing the herb chest, another boar sausage, his water skin, and the other half of the remaining cheese he'd hidden from the men. He then ran as quietly as he could to the tree gate and into the forest towards the shrine.

⟁

Uric made no movement nor sign that he'd heard Garen's approach, and when Garen arrived he understood why. Uric was sleeping a fever sleep, his breath labored and his skin burning to the touch, and dry.

Garen took off his tunic, poured some water on a sleeve, then twisted the edge of the linen and put it in Uric's mouth, hoping he'd suck at the water a little. Uric didn't respond to this, so Garen left it there and began looking at the blackening of his arm.

It looked really bad. The tourniquet had staunched the blood loss, but it could have done nothing to stop the spread of sickness further up his shoulder. Garen couldn't do anything for his arm, but he could clean out the wounds and mix something together to stop the spreading black.

He opened the chest and began searching for what would be needed. He couldn't boil the herbs and didn't have time to soak them in fire-water, but it would be enough if he chewed them himself and spit their essence into Uric's mouth.

Fortunately Yura had already extracted horsemint and branch-beard, so Garen started cleaning the open skin on Uric's arm with these and the other sleeve of his tunic while he chewed the bitter herbs. Uric started at the pain from Garen's scraping touch, but didn't open his eyes or speak. He did, however, bite down on the wet fabric and suck at it.

Garen kept chewing, and then clenched his teeth, used his fingers to pry open Uric's lips a bit, and let some spit drip from his mouth into Uric's. He then took a small sip of water and chewed more, and continued cleaning out the wound.

He kept at this, chewing, spitting, cleaning, then chewing, spitting, and cleaning again until he heard the snapping of a twig.

Garen stopped, stilled himself, and listened without moving. He heard more noise, a rustle of leaves, close to the shrine. Panic set in, and then just as quickly became something else, something he hadn't expected.

He raised himself up, standing calmly, and looked in the direction of the noise.

A man stood there, looking back at him. A bit older than Garen, darker hair, paler skin, silver and grey glinting in his beard, a hooded leather tunic of grey and brown open at his chest. He held a small axe in his right hand. His eyes, though, were what Garen noticed most: a pale, cold blue, the sky in winter.

The man stared at Garen. Garen stared back.

"You are hunting the last wolf." The man's voice was even: it seemed neither a question nor a statement.

Garen breathed. "The men with me are. I am not."

"The men with you will die."

Garen thought of Uric, then collected himself. "Who are you?"

"My name is not for you. The wolf will kill them. It may also kill you. Why are you here, if not to hunt the wolf?"

He squared his shoulders: "My name is Garen," he replied. "I'm a Provisioner. They compelled me to come with them, but I want to stop them."

"The man you are helping wishes harm to the wolf."

Garen looked down at Uric, who still had not awakened. Then he looked at the man again. "I can't let him die."

"Then the wolf will kill you, or I will kill you."

Garen sighed. "You speak for the wolf: again, who are you?"

"I speak for the wolf. He is the last wolf. Those here who protected him are dead."

Garen nodded. "The other men did that. And they will try to trap the wolf. I can try to stop them."

The man's face was expressionless. "Can you? Or will they kill you like those who tried to stop them before?"

Garen realised he didn't know the answer to that question. "I have something for you," Garen said instead, reaching into the small leather bag clasped to his belt. "It was given to me, but it belongs to the wolf."

He pulled out Yura's wolf paw from the bag and held it in front of him.

The man stared at the paw, and anger swept through his form. He raised his axe, and Garen was terrified. In this fear, however, the dreams came back to him: the woman, the hunter, the wound.

Garen understood. "It belonged to a she-wolf. A hunter cut it off, but I think she asked him to."

The man didn't answer except to growl, his axe still poised. Garen stared back at him, noticing he seemed reluctant or unable to step into the shrine.

"You can't come closer, can you?"

The man nodded.

Garen stepped forward. "I will come out to give this to you. You can attack me if you want, but please know: I want to stop the men I'm with from capturing you."

The man lowered his axe.

Garen stepped down from the shrine and put the wolf paw in the man's outreached hand. "I was told it happened over a hundred years ago."

Garen watched as the man stared at the paw in his hand. His face was inscrutable, betraying no emotion. He lifted the paw to his face, smelled it, then placed it quickly into a sack slung from his shoulder.

"How did you come by this?"

"A friend gave it to me. It came to her through her great-grandmother, who was given it by the hunter who cut it from the wolf."

Still the man's voice was even. "I know of the story by which he came by it. It was the paw of the second to last wolf."

Garen nodded. "I am sorry there is only one left. I want to try to help you stop them from taking the last wolf, too."

"I will kill them. First this man. Pull him out of the shrine."

Garen tensed. "The others are more your enemy. He can't kill you—he's sick and his arm is useless."

The man growled again. "One arm is enough to kill.'

Garen shook his head and stood fully upright, defiant. "If you kill him with my help, then I have killed him too. And I don't want to kill him."

The man snarled, then tilted his head to one side. "They are coming. I leave now."

"Wait!" Garen started to say, not because he wanted the man to stay but because he wanted to go with him. But it was anyway too late: the man ran, fast, into the thicker trees beyond the shrine.

Garen watched him until he could not see him anymore, then turned and froze. Ronúr, Huwvyn, and Thalyn were walking up the path, their weapons drawn. They couldn't have seen the man from where they were, but they could see Garen perfectly.

"Provisioner!" Ronúr shouted. "I told you to stay at the abbey."

Garen faced the approaching men, still far enough away that he could not see their expressions but too close for his two legs to run from them. He couldn't flee, but hadn't thought yet of a lie he could tell them. They would find Uric, and find Uric with him.

He tried the truth: "I found Uric. Something attacked him, but he's alive."

The three men broke their gait into a run towards him at Garen's words. Ronúr arrived first, and Garen pointed to Uric's fevered body on the wooden floor of the shrine. Ronúr looked at the man, then grabbed Garen's throat with his left hand and began crushing it.

"You traitor," Ronúr shouted, then hit Garen in the head with the hilt of his sword. Before the world went black, Garen heard him say, "you've been playing us the entire time."

CHAPTER FIFTEEN

He dreamed of a tree, a great yew. Blood dripped from its crimson berries, its roots gnarled, whitened bone protruding from the earth. Where the blood dripped into the dark soil sprung new saplings, their bright green needles giving off their own light.

Garen heard a rustle, and then a whimper. A beast padded through, grey and silver and black, sniffing at the earth. Then it dug with its forepaws and gnawed on a root until it cracked in its teeth. Blood poured out like sap from its marrow, running in little rivulets down the animal's maw.

It was the wolf, lapping up the yew's poison hungrily, crunching wood and bone in its teeth, swallowing great draughts of the tree's toxic ichor.

Garen tried to tell it no, to warn it, but no voice came. Instead, the branches of the yew quivered, shook in an unfelt wind, releasing the spirits of the dead like birds from its bower.

He tried to speak again. Again no voice came. Needles of yew fell from somewhere high in the tree. He looked up past those branches and saw stars, a night full of them, their light burning coldly from distant dreams.

The wolf moved, shifted its attention. Now it padded towards the trunk, scratched at its bark. It gnawed. Pieces fell off, exposing not soft wood but flesh, the bark peeling like skin from flesh. The tree quaked as the wolf clawed further, deeper, tearing out muscle and vein.

The wolf howled.

Garen writhed and screamed in pain.

"He's awake again," he heard. It was Thalyn's voice.

"Soon" came a gruff reply, Ronúr's growling timbre.

Garen tried to look around him but the pain was excruciating, paralyzing. Searing heat ran through his back, coursing up and down his spine, burning into an ice chill in his shoulders. From his chest came another pain, but different. The torment in his back felt metallic, but the agony across his chest felt like nettle, millions of barbs pricking his skin from his sternum to his groin.

He tried to see, but his eyes were wet, veiled in sweat or tears or blood. He tried to shift his body but the pain exploded again. He tried to kick, but his feet could not find the ground.

Words again, this time from Uric. "It's getting closer."

Uric was alive then. Hope suddenly opened a space through

the agony of his body, briefly clearing his mind. "Help me!"

Ronúr laughed. "Yeah too late for that, boy. But keep whimpering and I might fuck your corpse."

Garen writhed more, kicked his feet, flailed his arms. He touched nothing except empty air, heard the rattle of chain, felt the harrowing in his back. He suddenly understood what they'd done to him. He was strung up like a butchered animal, hanging by a chain from a tree, snared on the device Ronúr had carried. Its blades were hooked deep into the thick muscles of his upper back, just under his shoulders.

The hook in his back stopped him from raising his arms. His hands could never reach his face, so Garen blinked, then blinked again, trying to clear his eyes. He could see nothing but shapes, silhouettes, dim morning light, a distant flicker of orange flame.

They were not far from the abbey then, if that was still the fire in front of the gateyard. If so then they were close to the forest with the shrine, where Garen had found Uric and had met the wolf.

And just as he thought of the wolf, he heard the howl again.

Ronúr called out. "Huwvn, you see it yet?"

"Fuck," came the man's voice in return. "No. This is stupid. It'll kill us like it killed Jord."

"Coward," Thalyn spat. "We should have strung you up too."

Garen tried to listen past their arguing, but he could hear nothing else. He still could barely see, and the pain was becoming unbearable again. He didn't know if he could stay conscious any longer, and didn't know if he wanted to. The wolf was coming, and he was hooked to a chain, unable to defend himself, unable to flee.

Just then, he understood the fierce pain running across the skin of his chest and stomach. They'd carved a rune there, the same rune on the lock of the chest, the rune in the shape of the hook from which they'd hanged him. And from this, he understood why they'd done it.

The wolf was coming for him. They'd baited a runic trap with bloody, still-living flesh—his flesh. He was not just strung up on a wolf-trap.

He was the wolf-trap.

He was hanging from the yew he'd seen before waking to this torment. The rune was the yew, but bent wrong and barbed. The tree of death, of graveyards, of decay that nourishes life, the gate through death that leads to life.

Thorned now, and barbed: *a sacrificial yew.*

Garen was a sacrifice then, not just bait, but he did not know to whom. Not to the wolf, nor to any gods he knew. He could think of no god that would accept the unwilling offering of a man already devoted to another god, especially not to She-Who-Foresees.

"They're all afraid of her," Yura had once told him. "All the other gods. I ain't, but they are. She knows their futures and doesn't tell, holds them close to Herself. They say if She didn't exist, all the futures of the world and the gods would be unwritten—taken off the page if you get my meaning—and their pasts with them..."

"You needed a Provisioner for this," Garen groaned loudly, trying to bite back the pain. "What are you un-making?"

He hadn't really expected Ronúr to answer, but he did anyway. "The king is dying and his heir is a drooling idiot. It's time for a new sovereign."

Ronúr meant to take the power of the wolf to himself. That's why he didn't care about the lost horses: he had no intention of bringing the wolf back down the mountain. Maybe Uric had intended the same. Garen couldn't see Uric, wanted to scream at him for help.

Uric had only spoken once, and his voice betrayed no hint of a plan to save him. Garen understood, and all the hope he'd felt knowing Uric was alive drained out of him like the blood running down his back. If Uric meant to bring the wolf back to Arras, he would need to trap the wolf. And the only way to do that was for Garen to die.

Despair settled into the deepest parts of Garen's soul. Uric was not on his side at all. Uric had lied to the others, and had lied to Garen. Suddenly Garen understood—Uric must have known who Garen was the night they met in the docks, the night they fucked. He was a spy for Arras, hidden in plain sight in the king's bodyguards. It was probably easy for him to discover who the chosen Provisioner was, to meet that Provisioner the night before he was summoned.

But this didn't explain why Garen himself had been there at the docks, why She-Who-Foresees had sent him blindly like that. Unless...unless She had intended for Garen to know Uric was not who he said he was.

Garen traced this thought further: yes, this was it. Without meeting him before, Garen would never have confronted Uric, and Uric would never have had reason to reveal to Garen that he was a saboteur.

He almost managed to laugh at this realization, but instead, wincing against the pain, said aloud, "hope Uric doesn't get to the wolf first like he did with me."

Ronúr grunted back, "shut up, boy."

"What do you mean?" Thalyn asked that question.

"He faked his death. That was boar blood. He's working for Arras. And he killed Veln."

Garen felt a hard blow to his side. "Fuck off boy," Uric said.

But Garen's words had already begun their effect. Huwvn spoke now, fury edging his voice. "You killed my brother?"

Garen couldn't see what was happening but the sounds of struggle were enough for him to guess. He heard a clang of metal, Huwvn's axe against Uric's blade.

And then a loud roar from Ronúr. "Stop it," he shouted. "The boy's lying."

Then Thalyn's voice. "No, I think he's right. Ronúr, why was Uric hiding out there? I told you--"

A loud wet thud interrupted Thalyn's words. Ronúr had hit him again.

This time, though, Garen could hear Thalyn fighting back. The two men struggled just as Uric and Huwvn did, their boots scuffling across the ground, grunts and shouts and then suddenly that howl again, this time so close that Garen thought he could almost hear the wolf's intake of breath after.

The fighting stopped. Everyone and everything went silent.

Then the wolf howled again.

"Fuck this," Garen heard Huwvn say, and the man started to run off. But just before his third pounding step there was another wet thud and the man fell to the ground.

"Uric—you?" Ronúr growled.

The wolf growled.

Huwvn moaned from the dirt.

Thalyn choked out a laugh. "I told you."

Garen could see nothing, but what he heard was terrible. The men were fighting, fist against bone, knee against chest, shouts of pain and roars of rage, and then the sound of metal through flesh, sinew sliced, bones broken, limbs snapped in directions they were never meant to go.

And then the wolf bit into Garen's leg, its fangs deep in the muscle of his right calf.

This new pain was too much. Blackness came for him, tugging him earthward, ripping limb and life into the waiting, blood-soaked soil.

CHAPTER SIXTEEN

Garen woke into the chill of morning, his body in torment. Everything burned, but burned like ice, like cold stone or steel. He opened his eyes. He saw nothing but light and shadow without form.

A voice near his ear spoke. "You are awake."

He inclined towards the voice, familiar but hard to place. "I'm dying."

"No. But you are not well."

Garen tried to lift his arms, to push up with by his hands from the cold ground. He couldn't move them. The moment he tried, his back lit up with searing fire.

"Don't move. You need to rest."

Garen relented, then tried to turn his head toward the voice. More pain came with even that feeble attempt, so he gave up.

"Where am I?"

"In a cave in the forest above the abbey. I moved you here. I pulled you down from the hook."

Garen could place the voice now. "You're the wolf's guardian. It bit me. Where is it? Did they kill it?"

The man paused before replying. "The wolf is alive. The others are gone. Two are dead, two ran away. One was the man you were protecting."

"Uric..." Garen replied, slowly. "Where is he?"

The man yawned. "He escaped. I heard him sound a horn. He called others. They are not far."

Men from Arras were on their way, then. Garen was too exhausted to panic. "They will try to capture the wolf."

"Yes," the man replied. "I will need your help."

Garen moaned. "I can't move. I'm useless."

"You have healing herbs. I found them in the abbey. I brought the chest here. I had to break the lock."

Garen immediately regretted how angry his reply was. "I can't fix this! Did you see what they did to me? There are no herbs on earth that can mend muscle that fast."

"You are a Provisioner. I heard you say this. I heard them say this. You can see fate and reweave it. You don't need herbs."

Garen sighed, calming. "I don't reweave fate. I just see what will happen and know how to be ready for it."

"Then you know how to be ready for this," the man replied, gruffly. "You clutch to despair like it is a root. But it is not a root, it is a broken branch the tree no longer needs."

The man's words sounded like wisdom, ancient, calming, true. But they changed nothing: Garen still could not move, could not heal himself fast enough to be ready to fight. He couldn't even lift his head or arms.

"Can you help me?" Garen asked, finally.

"I have already. I will now. What do you need?"

"I need to dull this pain some. Can you read?"

"No. But I know many herbs by smell, though maybe not your names for them."

Garen breathed in deeply. "That will work. I will describe them. You will need hot water."

"I took your pot from the abbey. I can build a small fire here. There is enough wind the smoke will not give us away. I will clean you also. You smell like rot."

Garen almost managed a laugh. "Thanks."

He hadn't realised he'd passed out again until the man woke him. "The water is ready. What herbs are needed?"

Garen named them. The man only knew one of those names, so Garen then began to describe them as best he could.

"Just tell me their smells," the man said.

"Some of them have no odor," Garen replied.

The man grunted. "All plants smell. But maybe your nose is not good enough."

Garen sighed. "Maybe. I mean many of them smell the same."

The man grunted now. "Nothing smells the same. But tell me what they look like, then."

Garen tried to describe what he needed, and then asked the man to hold the vial in front of Garen's face so he could read the label. Once the man had collected everything, Garen then explained to him how to crush them, in which proportions, and how long to boil them.

The man's hostility from their meeting at the shrine was gone, replaced by an almost boyish eagerness to help. He sometimes even made light jokes that Garen didn't quite understand, but he felt disarmed by them regardless.

"The water has boiled half down. It is ready then?"

Garen nodded, then winced from the pain it caused. "Yes. You have to cool it, and then pour it into the places the hooks were, and where the wolf bit me. I'll scream."

"Sorry," the man replied. "But if you scream they will hear. They put sticks in the mouths of dogs to make them stop howling. I will do that to you." Garen heard a warmth in the man's voice when he said this.

"Good idea, okay. The liquid will clean the wounds and dull the pain. Then you will have to pour clear water over it, but wait until I stop trying to scream."

"Yes," the man said. "I will turn you over now."

The man pulled off the fur he had lain over Garen's naked body and paused, making a slight noise.

"The rune?" Garen asked, guessing what had drawn the man's attention.

"Yes...the rune," the man replied. "Ready? Here is a stick."

Garen opened his mouth to answer, but the stick was in between his teeth before the words came out. There was nothing else to do then but wait out the pain, so he gripped the wood in his mouth tightly.

The man rolled him over slowly with a care that feel like that of a parent with their child. Despite that light touch, however, the pain heaved through Garen's back as if the wounds were made anew.

Garen writhed against it, biting harder to stop from screaming, knowing that the worst had not yet begun.

The man poured the herb water into the wounds, and every thought, every memory, ever feeling inside Garen broke and howled against its leash of flesh. He saw stars, and light, and colors that didn't exist, his soul flying above the agony of his body, and through it.

The man was being careful, Garen knew it, but nothing felt kind. He wanted to lash out, to gnaw at the man, rip off his skin with teeth in retaliation for the pain. But the pain wasn't from the man, Garen knew this also. Anyway, Garen could do none of those things with his body broken like this.

Garen followed the scattered thoughts, the fury and the torment, back into his body. A kind of euphoria began to settle there, slowly, his body recoiling now not from the pain but from sense itself.

The herbs were working, then. Garen let them the work, floated a bit above their touch, warming where had been ice, cooling where had been fire.

Forgetting the stick in his mouth, Garen tried to speak. He could form no words, could move neither his teeth nor tongue with the wood in the way.

"I will take the stick out now. You are not trying to scream anymore."

Garen felt the man's fingers in his mouth for a moment, and then nothing in his mouth besides what was part of it.

"Thank you," Garen said, whimpering a little.

"I will wash you now. The water is warm. There was soap in your pack."

Garen felt like he was floating no longer on air but on water, and he sank into the feeling as he felt the man's fingers carefully rinse out his wounds. His body didn't respond with pain but merely eager submission to the water and the man's touch.

"I never got your name," Garen said.

"Lorn," the man replied. "You are Garen. You told me this."

"Lorn...abandoned."

"Yes," the man replied. "Alone. You understand that, I think."

Garen shifted his head slightly. With the herbs coursing into his blood, it did not hurt to move it, though it had not been only the pain which had prevented him earlier. "Yes. I guess I do."

Lorn poured more warm water on Garen's back, and Garen embraced the sensation as it dripped down his sides.

"How long have you guarded the wolf?" he asked.

Lorn's hands moved down Garen's back to his waist, massaging in more soaped water. "My entire life. There is no one else. I am the last one."

"Like the wolf," Garen replied, then quivered. Lorn's hands had moved even further down, were now lightly scrubbing inside the cleft of his ass.

"This is okay?" the man asked, slightly pausing.

"Ye...yes."

The man started again. "You seem to like it."

Garen answered breathlessly. "I do."

"It is not fair of me, maybe. Your body is broken. You could not stop me if you wanted to."

"I don't want you to stop."

The man stopped for a moment, then said, "I want more. I should stop."

"No. More is fine. But I cannot return the kindness yet."

The man stood up suddenly. "You do not understand. It is not kindness. I would not be able to stop."

Garen wanted to laugh, but he stopped himself. The man was obviously tormented by something. "You've done this before?" he said, instead.

"No."

"You are right. I don't understand."

Garen could hear the man walk away, and then return. "I cannot undo it."

Garen was even more confused now. "Undo what? What are you not telling me?"

The man knelt down over Garen's body, his knees straddling his chest. "I do not guard the wolf."

"Oh," Garen said, suddenly understanding. "You *are* the wolf."

"Yes. It was I who bit you. I'm sorry. The rune made me. And I do not know if it is the rune that makes me want you so much now."

"You're also human, though."

"Yes. We all were. And also wolf. And I am the last."

"That's why you were so angry when I gave you the wolf paw."

The man shifted down along Garen's body. "That was my mother's."

Garen felt drugged by the herbs, but his mind still worked enough to understand this made no sense. "You mean great-grandmother? It's over a hundred years old. It couldn't be your mother's."

The man growled, tersely. "I know my mother's scent. She died not long after I was born, but I know her scent." Then the man's voice softened. "I see. We do not age like you do. Sorry to be angry."

Garen started to answer but shuddered instead. Something warm and wet ran along the cleft of his ass. Not the man's hands, but his tongue, exploring hungrily.

"Ah..." Garen finally managed to say in reply. "That feels good."

"I told you I should stop. I cannot undo it."

Garen was feeling teased. He asked again. "Undo what?"

The man stopped again. "You would become wolf."

"Oh! So Uric and Ronúr both had it wrong. You don't fuck the wolf for sovereignty, the wolf fucks you."

Lorn grunted and laughed. "They think the wolves made kings? No. We only make wolves like us. Kings have captured wolves, made them do to them against their will what all of my body now wants to do to you. With will."

Garen tried to parse this all out, trying to hold back his own desire long enough to understand. "Anyone who has sex with a wolf becomes one too?"

"No. That is how a man-wolf makes another wolf. The she-wolves, like my mother, they bore wolves. If the mate was a wolf too, her child would always be a wolf. If he was only a man, then only sometimes would she bear a wolf. She would bear a wolf more often in times of fear or pain."

Garen remembered the recurring dream. The woman, pregnant, laying on furs. The man, Yura's great-grandfather, cutting off the woman's hand at the wrist.

"That is why your father cut off your mother's hand?"

Lorn sighed. "Yes. To make sure I would be a wolf."

"I'm sorry," Garen said.

"It was her choice. I don't know if I would have made the same. If I knew my child would be alone..."

In a brief moment, the deep despair Lorn must have felt the last hundred years hit Garen like a stone in the stomach. "When did she die?"

"Not long after I was born. Men from the cities came for her. She killed herself before they could take her. They did not know she had a child."

Garen wanted to hold the man, but he could not move. "I'm so sorry."

Lorn paused, then continued. "The people in the abbey raised me. They are why I survived. But they are gone now, killed. And the people in the villages, also dead."

"One of their murderers are dead now, too," Garen replied, thinking of Jord. "But that does not bring them back."

Lorn made a noise, like he had choked perhaps. It came again, and again, and Garen understood: Lorn was crying.

"I'm sorry," Garen said, wishing his arms worked so that he could hold him.

Lorn sobbed, then suddenly quieted. "I cannot undo it, if I do it. And I would do it because I am selfish. Because I want you. I also do not want to be alone. But also..."

Garen waited, but Lorn didn't continue. "But also what?"

"It might heal you. We heal fast. That is how we live so long.

This is why kings want us, to heal faster, to live longer. If I do this, you would heal fast. But I cannot undo it. You will become wolf, and live long. Too long maybe, like I have, alone."

"This is a lot," Garen said, slowly, weighing his words. "But for you it seems harder than for me. Provisioners see their death, and I have never seen mine. This is probably why. For me this is not a hard choice. I have only one true friend, and she was the one who gave me your mother's hand. I think she saw this would happen. There are no others who would miss me or even know I was gone.

"But also," Garen continued, "when I saw you at the shrine you looked familiar. Like I already knew you, or knew you later and remembered in the past. That has never happened before. And Yura said that is what love is like, so maybe I love you and I don't know it yet. I have never known love, but maybe I will."

"I don't know love either," Lorn said. "There was a man once, one of the guardians. I thought I loved him. And I think he wanted to love me, and maybe I wanted to love him. But it was forbidden—the guardians could not, would not, mix with the wolves. It was their pact with the BearFather, the god who made us too."

"Ah," Garen said. "The god of the shrine. We call him Matu, the Magician-King. But he has other names."

"Many," Lorn said. "And he is not kind, but also I guess not unkind."

Garen laughed, remembering how Yura once said the same thing of She-Who-Foresees. "Gods are not much different from us."

"No," Lorn sighed. "But it was forbidden, and it felt unkind, but maybe it was also kind. So I did not know love, and the man is gone now like all the others."

Garen didn't have time to measure his words, so quickly they came. "I'm here now. I would like to stay with you. I want to feel you, and feel like you do. And I want to protect you when the men come."

Lorn's voice lowered, a timbre that felt more animal than human. "I want this too. I want you. I..."

Garen heard a sound he thought he would never forget, a guttural, snarling growl. "What's happening?"

"I cannot stop it. I'm sorry."

Garen tried to turn his head to look at Lorn's face, but the deep wounds from the hooks, wounds that had severed muscle, stopped him. Instead he spoke. "Don't be sorry. I want this."

"I..." Lorn said, snarling. "I want you."

Garen felt forest inside him, and stone. Steep cliffs crowned with fir and pine, cascades tumbling down from their edges from melting winter snows. He felt wood inside him, and rock, dark soil and root thrust deep into all that made him human.

He heard Lorn growling, heard his guttural voice snarl, grunt, gnarr with every movement. He felt hot skin and sweat and hair, and then fur, and then skin again. The man's hands clutched Garen's, their fingers entwined. Garen looked and they were great grey paws, then hands again, then something in between.

The man, or the wolf, or the man-wolf bellowed, howled,

groaned, gnawed at Garen's neck, ran his tongue across Garen's skin, hot and wet and coarse. He heaved into Garen, driving harder. Each time he went deeper in, Garen felt less human, less singular, less a mere self. He was the vast webs of fungus across ancient wealds, the vast threads of streams veining into rivers and into the sea.

And then Lorn howled again, a deep quaking wail, feral, virile, brutal but with a tone of sweetness, of care, of love. Garen took his heat into him, felt himself filled, felt himself as a dried ravine swollen suddenly with autumnal rains.

Lorn howled again, then growled, and rolled off of Garen's body onto his side. Garen could see him this way, and looked, expecting to see the beast, the wolf who'd fucked him. But he saw only the man instead, sweat soaking his thick brow, beard, and hair.

"You're beautiful," Garen said. "I think I will fall in love with you."

Lorn stared back at him, a confused, exhausted, but tender regard. "Sorry if I was rough. I don't...I've never done this."

Garen smiled. "I would never have guessed that. Next time I'd like to see you when we do this."

Lorn was silent for a brief moment. "Something is different. I think it is the rune. I became man again too fast, against my will. It happened too when I bit you, when you were on that hook. I was wolf, and then I wasn't. I didn't choose it."

"You chose this, though? I mean, to fuck me?"

Lorn nodded, still gazing into Garen's eyes. "Yes. With all of me. You did too?"

"With all of me, yes." Fighting back a sudden exhaustion, Garen yawned, then asked, "what now?"

"I don't know. I have never done this. I do not know how the change happens, or how fast." He ran his fingers along Garen's jaw, tracing his sparse beard from ear to chin and then back again. "You will make a good wolf, I think. But..." he said, his voice suddenly shaken, "I should not have howled. I am now worried. They might find us here."

Garen yawned again, then tried to move his body. No pain came, thanks still to the herbs, but he still could not turn his head, move his shoulders, or shift his body.

"Don't try to move yet," Lorn said, moving his face closer to Garen's. "You should sleep. You will be safe. I will protect us both."

CHAPTER SEVENTEEN

You must wake up.

They were running across leaves, jumping over roots, crashing through ferns, low young pines and cedars. They splashed into and over rivulets and streams, scrambling up hills following deer and elk tracks between massive yellow-lichened stone.

Every step brought to his nose new shocks of senses, smells more varied and meaningful than the colored world of light upon which his eyes had long learned to rely. Lorn had been right: every plant had an odor. Fern was fragrant in a way different from ivy, both different from the perfume of moss, lichen, and sedge. The rot of old leaves in stagnant pools smelled, as did the mud, as did sun-warmed stone, mushrooms and molds, all mixing but never lost into the sweeter smells of pine and cedar sap. And then there were the animal smells, the faint wet musks of boar and rat, lower odors than the salt-sweet sweat of deer and rabbit. Somewhere there was honey in a tree, ravens tearing apart the half-decomposed corpse of a spent salmon at the end of its journey.

Sounds, too, exploded around them, vibrating, trembling, shaking the earth in all directions, wind amplifying and muting distant calls, crashes, creaks, splashes of water against rock, dance of leaf against leaf, call of bird and wail of beast —an endless symphony both lush and disorienting. The world was alive in ways more immediate and more present than Garen had ever before understood.

Only the change in his vision made this new intensity tolerable. Color had faded, greens greyed as in the gloaming dimness after sunset, distant shapes indistinguishable until they were just in front of him. To his eyes the world around him was drenched in the fog of dreaming, while to his ears and nose the world was sharp and urgent.

You must wake up.

They were running, not from nor towards. They were running to run, to move through the forests, through the world, just to be moving through it. Like swimming, immersed in the desire of movement itself, movement without desire of arrival.

He did not want to ever stop. He could run alongside Lorn forever, chasing his tail, smelling his musk, listening to his panting breath, hearing the soft padding thud of his paws against the moist earth, slowing only long enough to sniff the air, to find some new whim to chase before chasing another, and another, and another.

There was something new on the air, new animal scents: two. One he recognized too well, the acrid, sour smell of city men. The other, though—an animal bigger than all the others, musty, old, scent of wet grass, berries, strong muscle. He did not know this odor yet.

Lorn slowed even more, then stopped. Garen didn't want to stop running, but he would not run without Lorn, so he slowed and stopped too.

He growled, and Garen understood "men." Another growl, and Garen understood "bear."

You must wake up.

Lorn licked Garen's face, nipped his jaw, then his ear. It felt warm, loving, playful, but Garen smelled fear on him.

They both sniffed the air again, then Lorn leapt into a run again. Garen followed his lead but didn't understand, wanted to pull him back, lead Lorn instead in a different direction. Lorn was running from the smell of the bear, towards the smell of men. This was wrong, the wrong destination. The bear could protect them from the men, Garen thought. The men would kill them.

You must wake up.

Lorn ran faster and faster, and Garen struggled to follow him. Before, they had run without destination, neither from nor towards, completely without fear. Now they were running from something, running towards another thing, and none of this seemed right.

Garen stopped and howled at Lorn, howled for him to stop too. But Lorn didn't stop, didn't even turn his head. He continued, kept running, crashing faster and faster through the underbrush of the forest, down from the heights they had climbed towards, into the lower lands where men made their homes and wars.

Garen howled again, but Lorn was gone from his vision and fading from his hearing. Only his scent remained, still on his face and in the air before him.

He wanted to follow him, chase after him, stop him from running into death. And he started, but something else was suddenly close, a strong odor, a heat, a rushing noise.

Garen stared at the massive bear in front of him and cowered, yelping. It stood on its hind legs, towering above him, blotting out the light.

Garen whined. The bear spoke.

"You must wake up."

Garen woke, groaning in pain. The numbing of the herbs had worn off and he felt sick from the dull ache wracking through his body.

He felt cold, the chill of the stone under the furs upon which he'd slept draining his heat. He turned his head, shuddering in the pain he'd forgotten would come. His neck worked though, enough to see that Lorn was not there next to him.

"Lorn?" he called out. Only his own voice answered him, echoing off the stone of the cave.

Garen tried to get up, to stand. But he couldn't move more than his neck or his legs. His back felt frozen, paralyzed from the severed muscles, pain screaming at him each time he tried.

He called out again, then tried to roll over before blacking out from the shock of pain that seared through him.

"You must wake up." The bear spoke again, growling in a voice that felt like the sound of the forest itself, or of stones laughing on mountainsides and rain pouring through them.

"Lorn is gone," Garen growled back to the bear. "I do not want to wake without him."

"He is not returned to the roots of the world. He is not gone as you mean it."

Garen understood. "You are Matu."

The bear rose up even taller, then just as suddenly returned all four legs back to the ground. "Magician-King to your kind, Bear-King to others, the Unafraid One to still more. But you are Hers whom even I fear."

Despite his sorrow, despite his confusion, despite all the terror of Matu's presence, Garen smiled for a moment. He thought of Yura shouting at She-Who-Foresees, the Lady of the Provisioners, of whom even other gods were afraid.

"I am, yes," Garen answered. "Where is Lorn?"

"Men have him, men who know no gods but themselves."

Despair choked in Garen's throat, his voice a whining moan of a pup rather than that of a wolf. "Uric…"

"They will take his power, which is my power. They want to become gods."

Garen's voice returned stronger. "Lorn is yours?"

"I made his ancestors, so he is mine."

"Does that make me yours now, too?"

The bear roared angrily. "No. But you have also my power now, though it was not meant for you. But you will serve me."

Garen snarled in rage. "I will not serve you. But I will save Lorn."

The bear snarled back. "You may not be able to save him."

The uncertainty of this ancient god shook the core of Garen's soul. "I will try. I will try with all of me."

The bear snarled again. "They will take his power, which is my power. They will become as gods, and bring death to the gods, even to her whom you serve, the Star-Weaver Herself."

Garen had never heard this name for Her, but felt its truth immediately. "That is why She sent me here, then. But men cannot kill gods."

The roar the bear made sounded like bitter laughter. "You are a stupid man, then. You cannot see what we hold back from the world. All men are stupid, and cannot see this. If they become as gods, they will not hold it back. They will invite it in, remake the world to welcome it. And they will choke us out, starve us, chase us to our deaths like they chased the wolves."

Garen smelled acrid, black smoke, heard clashing din of rhythmic metal. He heard forests scream until they fell forever silent, watched great rivers slow, then choke, then drain away into parched corpse dirt.

He understood nothing of what he saw, or heard, or smelled as the bear spoke, but he felt it all true. "Then I will stop them."

"Hear me again. You must kill them. You may not save Lorn, nor even yourself, but you must not let them take my power."

Garen growled back at the bear. "Lorn will not die, nor will the gods, nor will I. But this is your fault, isn't it? You gave your power to wolves knowing humans could steal it from them."

The bear reared up on its hind legs again and looked ready to maul Garen. "You are a stupid, stupid man. You are Hers, or I would kill you. You cannot understand, and this story is not for you."

Garen didn't cower. "Then I will learn it from Her. But tell me —which of the men I was with survived?"

The bear relented its rage. "The two who have been in you as Lorn was."

"Uric. And Ronúr. Which took Lorn?"

"They are taking him north, not from where you came."

Garen nodded. "Arras. So Uric has him. But Ronúr is alive. I will find them."

The bear spoke evenly, almost kindly. "The rune will slow you. You will not change as Lorn does, unless you can gain its power."

Garen nodded. "Then I will gain it."

The bear approached Garen, its great maw near Garen's face. "Your body is broken. You will heal. Faster than a man but not yet like Lorn. But you do not have time to heal. You must wake up."

Garen woke.

Rhyd Wildermuth

Rhyd is a druid, a theorist, and a writer.

His non-fiction books include *Your Face Is A Forest, A Kindness of Ravens, Witches In A Crumbing Empire*, and *All That Is Sacred Is Profaned*, all available from Gods&Radicals Press / Ritona a.s.b.l (abeautifulresistance.org).

He lives in the Ardennes, a short walk from where the last wolf of Luxembourg was killed in the 19th century and where corpses of sheep gnawed by a wolf were found in 2020.

One recent starry evening, he heard that wolf howl.

Find his writing at RhydWildermuth.com

RITONA